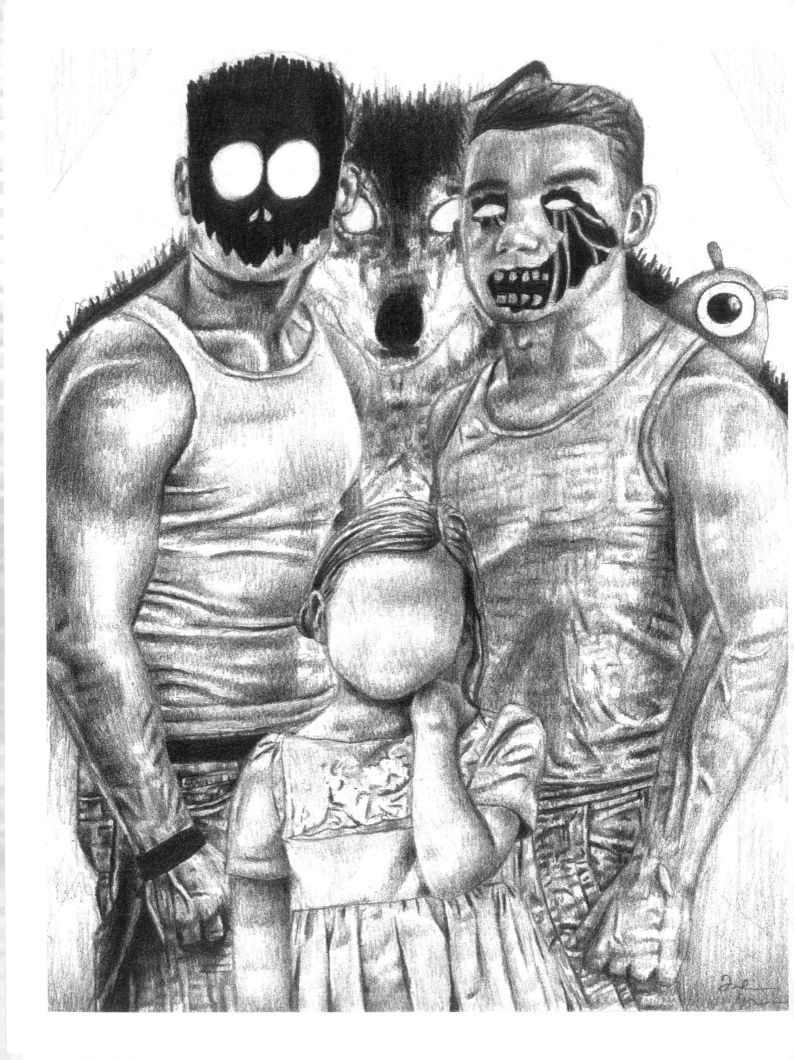

# TABLE OF CONTENTS

*cover art by Adam Miller*
*table of contents art by Jacob Carignan*

# FOREWORD

At the intersection of cryptozoology and folklore, the legendary local monster finds its place in the American psychogeographic landscape. Such monsters inhabit a kind of hallucinatory paradox: feared and desired, hunters and hunted, unbelievable but believed. They come to life through the words of storytellers who, like snake handling Adventists, mix up pure faith with selective evidence, fine language with fanged beasts. The monster apostles whisper tales in backwoods and stripmalls, retell stoned thirdhand accounts in Taco Bell Drive-ins and gas station lines and clapboard bait-and-tackle shops. They believe, they believe. The creatures are out there.

But in this book the snakes have been taken from the parishioners and given over to a wholly unqualified cohort of new handlers, off-kilter men and women who approach the monstrous menagerie with lust instead of terror, who aestheticize the blood, the bulge-eyes, the rough half-human voices. Our uncautious chroniclers have dragged these beasts from the relative safety of remote rural hollows and fetid swamps choked with ghostly epiphytes, amplified the creatures' most grotesque features and put them on display in this half-accurate atlas of American bogeymen.

The cries of seductive frogs and skinning bunnymen echo across these pages. There are weepers and creepers, thunderbirds, well-hung feral apemen, and a snarky talking grundle, among other deadly denizens of regional myth.

So you'll read these tales and feel the little thrill of contained fright. You'll maybe cross off a few regions on your US map, unsafe spots, territories you'll cede to these terrors. But you'll forget soon enough. You'll plan a camping trip and wind up in heart of the pine barrens. But you'll be safe then. Or probably.

The real danger is that, by the time you finish reading, the monsters in this book—miniature versions of them, microscopic Maine Beasts and Green Men and the like—will have already lodged themselves in your kidneys. They'll have carved out little rooms, furnished them with mid-century futons, green Tiffany desk lamps. They will be waiting. They will hitch a ride with you until you have children and then switch over to your progeny. And they will grow inside your babies until they're ready to crawl from your child's mouth—perhaps she will be 2 or 3 years old—and out toward your face.

A six inch chupacabra on your toddler's tongue. That's what's coming. Or worse. And there won't be any escape. The state of terror is permanent.

—*Ben Segal*

# THE WEST

UTAH ◼ THE SKINWALKER RANCH
## High Desert Climate


NEW MEXICO ◼ LA LLORONA
## La Llorona, She Weeps With You


ARIZONA ◼ CHUPACABRA
## Guerilla


CALIFORNIA ◣ THE SPACE BRAIN
## Take the Time to Understand Yourselves


COLORADO ◼ THE SLIDE ROCK BOLTER
## A Mythical Terrestrial Cetacean as Deus Ex Machina Or, Dave McCormick Finally Gets What's Coming to Him

# HIGH DESERT CLIMATE

## Ryan Bradford

*"In June of 1996, a story appeared in the Desert News, Salt
Lake City's second largest newspaper....According to the
article, Tom and Ellen Gorman bought the ranch in the spring
of 1994. The Gormans were surprised by the deadbolt locks
both inside and outside of the doors. Even the windows were
bolted. There were huge metal rings at both ends of the house,
where large dogs had been chained. There was a strange clause
in the real-estate contract that there was to be no digging on
the ranch without notification of the previous owners. That
seemed to be 'a meaningless clause crafted by elderly
eccentrics.'"*

- Francis B. Salisbury, *The Utah UFO Display*

The second time I arrived at the cabin, I didn't know it was the second time. I felt
unwound from what the man showed me the first time, my mind in a state of disrepair.
Knuckles were sore from gripping the wheel. Jeep spat dirt. I soared over the rise and
saw an open field. The landscape painted black under a starry night. A single tree and
an illuminated window. Didn't even occur to me that the field, the house, the sky were
the same.

I ran to the door, pounded on it.

"Please open up," I shouted. "I need to find my wife."

The familiarity of the wood against my hand turned my insides. It was then that I realized that I had returned.

Impossible.

The same man opened the door.

"Hello," he said. "Would you like to see what is in my cabinet?"

I turned and fell off his porch. Scrambled back to the jeep. I might have screamed, but the man's laughter was all I could hear.

It was Loretta's idea to go on the hike.

"You look like you need some fresh air."

The sun had begun its descent when we reached the top of the hiking trail. I had watched Loretta's muscular calves the entire way up, knew that she was walking at a slower pace for my sake—a subtle act of mercy that quietly infuriated me.

We emerged at the summit. A welcome breeze blew through my drenched clothing, dried the hair that had been plastered to my forehead. I found a boulder where I could sit and catch my breath. I scraped a jagged, dry piece of snot out of my nose and was very satisfied at the clean integrity with which it emerged. *Perhaps the only positive aspect of these high desert climates,* I thought.

Loretta took a tiny sip of her water and offered it to me. I drank with lust, letting wetness dribble down my unkempt, scraggly face. Loretta turned away and admired the view. She put her hands on her hips, her arms winged out, defiant against any sign of physical exhaustion.

"Oh look at the sky! It's beautiful, right?" Loretta said. I rolled my eyes. "The Uinta mountains are the biggest range in the US that runs east to west," she said. I was tempted to pull out my phone to validate her claim, but realized I didn't really care. She turned to me, took the water bottle back. The emptiness of it made her frown. "I wish you'd come out here with me more often," she said. "It kills me to see you spending so much time in front of a screen."

It felt like she was repeating lines from a movie or a healthy living blog—an amalgam of the carpe diem-like slogans she posted ad nauseum to her social media feeds throughout the day, which I knew were aimed at me.

"Yeah, well, it's my job," I said, cutting myself off before I added something nasty.

Loretta walked to the other side of the peak. She put her hand over her eyes to shield the sun, braced herself against the wind, and for a brief moment I wanted to call her out on the overly dramatic pose.

I looked down and watched a lizard crawl across the ground by my shoe. Its movements were so quick that they looked disconnected, like a filmstrip with frames removed.

I heard Loretta call my name. "Come over here! Check this out." She pointed over the ridge at something I couldn't see from my vantage point. She put her hand over her mouth. I looked down at the lizard, who remained frozen, looking at me with tiny black eyes.

Then Loretta screamed. The sky darkened immediately and the earth produced a savage light. I fell to the ground. My eyes burned; the surrounding landscape appeared in negative. An overbearing low frequency shook the mountain. I opened my eyes briefly and saw three lights—each the size of my jeep—directly overhead, spinning erratically. Three miniature white suns spinning against the grotesque black sky.

Loretta's screaming broke through the wave of noise. I tried to get up off the ground, but felt pummeled by a sudden force from above. I looked around for her, but the landscape was too bright. Her screaming rose in pitch—unnaturally, as if her vocal cords were stretched longer than the human neck can accommodate—before cutting out entirely.

The lizard was dead when I woke up— it had died in its watchful position. Two empty sockets remained where its black eyes used to be. I poked it and it toppled over, retaining a crouched posture.

I sat up and screamed for Loretta. The brush shivered in the wind. I crossed my arms and rubbed my shoulders, still felt damp with sweat. I hadn't been out for too long.

I descended the trail with manic intent, occasionally screaming my wife's name. Branches scraped my face; rocks tripped me up. At one point, I stopped to catch my breath against a tree, resting my face directly on the knotty bark. I cried loudly, pounding the wood with my fist. I punched until I felt a soft mass hit me on the head and land at my feet. A crow stared back at me from the ground, its eyes burnt out the same way as the lizard.

Another dead bird dropped to my side, and another. Soon, the feathery corpses were raining down from the branches and collecting around the trunk. I turned, hurried along my way. The bottom of the sun touched the landscape by the time I got to the bottom.

I drove as fast along the mountain road as the vehicle could handle. The dirt provided little traction, and during a few perilous instances I thought I'd be tossed out into the rocky valley below. *Fine*, I thought, *let me be pummeled into dirt. Let no evidence of my existence remain.* But these thoughts were short-lived, and I felt ashamed of my own cowardice.

The first time I arrived at the cabin, the sky was light. That's what I kept coming back to—an anchor to ground my sanity. The brain is very adept at consoling the details and smoothing out the trauma. But the sky (*oh! the sky*) is an infinite that can't be forgotten.

The jeep cleared the rise. Caught air. The road leveled out and I looked upon the field, the tree, the cabin.

I ran up to the front door. Inseminated my hand with splinters with the first knock. Kept knocking.

The man who opened the door was so tall that the doorframe cut off the upper half of his face. He wore a black suit and a bolo tie adorned with silver and turquoise jewelry. His arms came down past his hips and swung toward me, knuckles-out, when he rested his forehead against the lintel. When he spoke, his jaw chattered in a manner discordant with the words fleeing it, similar to how an amateur ventriloquist would work a a puppet.

"Hello. Would you like to see what is in my cabinet?"

The adrenaline hadn't worn off; his greeting didn't register. My blood ran hot through my temples. "Do you have a phone?" I asked, pleaded. "I've had an emergency. I'm looking for my wife. I need to use your phone. Mine doesn't work." I held mine out for visual confirmation.

"Come in." He ushered me in with his giant pendulum hands and closed the door behind us. A scent touched my nostrils, simultaneously attractive and repulsive, like turning fruit. The darkness felt encompassing within his dwelling, rendering the twilight outside unbearably bright. I put palms in my eyes, foolishly rubbed to hasten their adjustment to the dark, and the pressure created purplish explosions in my vision. It was during that perversion of sight that the man moved from one side of the room to the other. I am almost certain that he scurried on all fours.

I blinked and the man appeared upright. His head rested high in the corner of the ceiling. His features shadowed. A creeping fear overtook the panic. I doubted he had a phone.

"My wife," I said. "She needs—"

"Please, look in the cabinet," he said. I hesitated for a moment before he placed a massive hand on my shoulder, despite his placement on the other side of the room. With arms that grew and shrunk to accommodate the navigation, he guided me around the table to a black, lacquered cupboard that I hadn't noticed before. Its ornate engravings and silver handles did not match the rustic—nearly primitive—décor of the cabin. A muffled scratching came from the other side of the door.

A crack of a match made shadows lean. He placed the match to a candle in his other hand. It was the first time I fully saw his face. His eyes shined from drooping, blackened depressions like a man wearing a loose mask.

He leaned down. "Open it," he said.

I held the handle. The scratching within intensified. I pulled.

The inside of the cabinet was not more than three feet wide and two feet deep. Yet somehow, Loretta was in there, tucked away in a middle shelf. The shape of the compartment had contorted her, flattened her at the sides like a forced piece of clay. A single eye, moist and fearful, watched me, framed by folds of impossible flesh. Her pinky was the only protrusion from her cubed body. It scratched upward in a hook. *C'mere* it gestured to me. The nail had broken from scratching the inside of the door.

*C'mere.*

I slammed the door to the cabinet. The man stood. His lips appeared to have melted together, and when he laughed, they pulled apart in strands. His mouth, a cavernous maw guarded by a skin cage.

That was the first time his laughter followed me off his porch.

I watched the miles tick away and the gas level drop from half a tank to a quarter to E. The jeep ran out of gas before clearing the next rise.

I hiked the summit on foot. Above, the moon had swelled yellow; a grotesque sky blister. It cast a sickly glow on the same field, the same drooping tree, the same cabin.

The terror felt electric. I turned and ran down the hill, the way from which I had come. I made it back to the jeep when a scaly trunk the size of a skyscraper dropped from the heavens and smashed the vehicle completely. The impact shook me off my feet. I lay on my back, deafened, and gazed upon the gargantuan monster. The trunk extended skyward for miles until it connected with a body that blacked out the sky. Another pillar swung forward and smothered an acre of forest on my opposite side. A reptile face lowered, connected to an elongated neck, emitted a scream of continuous thunder, and took a bite of the world. The dirt underneath my feet crumbled and fell into the chasm it created. I scrambled to my feet and ran back up the hill.

When I passed the cabin, the tall man was standing on the side of the street. The ugly moon shone on a false face smiling idiotically.

"Would you like to see what's in my cabinet?" he asked.

I held my hand to the side of my face, blocked him out of the peripheral, kept running.

It was no surprise that the field, tree and cabin were over the next rise. My journey had been marked by a series of rises and plateaus, and I resigned to the idea that I'd never reach the apex. I turned off the road and up the driveway leading to the cabin. A dark shape crossed in front of the lit window and waved to me.

When I knocked on the door, Loretta answered.

I searched for words, but was dumbfounded. My knees gave out. I fell and she caught me, dragged me into the cabin and set me onto the floor. I tasted water on my lips, took the bottle from her hands and drank until it was gone.

"I was so worried about you," she said. "Where did you go?"

A residual drop of water slid down my throat wrong. I sputtered. "What do you mean?"

Loretta's brow furrowed. Her lips became a concerned line. "We were up on the mountain. The sky lit up—" She paused. "I've never seen anything like it before. Then you were gone."

"I was there. I've been looking for you too." My body ached and my appendages felt heavy like they were filling with cement. My eyes fluttered.

Loretta stroked my hair and leaned down to my ear. "Shhh, don't worry about it. We're together now." She kissed me. She tasted like rotting fruit.

"Where are we?" I asked.

"I found this cabin. It's so beautiful here. You should really see what's in this cabinet."

"The cabinet," I said.

She didn't respond, but looked at me with drooping eyes. I pulled her in for another kiss. The skin on her face was waxy and loose. I felt it slide off her face and drop onto mine, where it lay like an inside-out mask. I pushed her off.

"I will never look in that cabinet," I said and wrapped my hands around her throat. I dug my thumbs into her esophagus and squeezed until my fingers interlocked. She raised her claws (oh god) and tore strips off my hands. Blood made my grip slippery. I pressed harder. She thrashed. I screamed. She died.

I held her neck for another five minutes before letting go. I replaced her face, laying the skin down gently and kneading it at the edges.

"Beautiful," I said.

A deep rumbling shook the floor. The candle flickered. I had to hurry. I took hold of Loretta's hair and dragged the body to the front door. I glanced at the cabinet before pulling her down the steps.

The walk was difficult; Loretta's body did not slide easily over the dirt. I distracted myself by practicing lines that I would say to the man in the cabin upon my next arrival.

*You've got something to show me? Well, have I got something for YOU.*

I had to rest multiple times on the trek up the rise. I walked backwards, holding her hair with both hands—a perpetual game of tug-o-war. Excitement welled in me.

I fell backwards when we hit the summit, not expecting the level ground. The dirt felt nice. I screamed my laughter at the descending moon. Birds chirped their morning salutations. I sat up on my elbows and turned my head.

The cabin was gone. There was no field. The road continued forward and down before ending abruptly, swallowed by the flora that covered the other side of the mountain. I rubbed my eyes, created more purple explosions, let the shapes dance as I scoured the landscape. We were at such a great height. I pulled Loretta up from the slope, sat her next to me so we could enjoy the view together. We watched the sunrise.

Then I stood, took her by the hair again and dragged her to where the road ended. We pushed into the forest. It was slow going, but we would eventually hit another rise. I hoped there was another rise.

# La Llorona, She Weeps With You

## Julia Dixon Evans

*"Of all the variations heard today, the most popular one conjures up an image of the modern La Llorona in a black or white cloak...wandering the arroyos, acequias and riverbeds, weeping and wailing for her lost children. Whether these children have been lost, accidentally drowned, or murdered outright by their infamous mother depends upon the storyteller."*

- Judith S. Beatty and Denise M. Lamb, *La Llorona*

My name is Ceanothus. My mother named me after a plant that grows in her old home in the high coastal deserts of California. It's technically a bush, but to my mother it was always a tree.

"He'd grow them to be sixteen, seventeen feet high, taller than the roof," she'd say, late at night when neither of us could sleep in the heat.

"I loved the lilac blooms," she'd say. "I loved the way they lit up the entire tree, the way it blossomed at the tail end of what never even felt like winter in the first place."

Sometimes she would tell me she loved sitting with her father, just the two of them, counting the clusters of petals. She'd clutch his opera glasses, weird, shiny binoculars, to her face and watch zoomed-in birds hop around in the upper branches. In April they would prune the *ceanothus* together, a gardenful of veins.

"He always called them trees," she'd say, and she'd smile at me and kiss my face, but most of the time she didn't speak about him. "I want you to grow tall and live for a hundred years."

She moved out here after an argument eleven years ago, after I was born. I don't think her father ever wanted her to leave, but those are the words he used anyway. She drove me, her baby boy, all the way to New Mexico in one day, and has not spoken to her father since.

I have two things from my grandfather: my name, and his opera glasses. And I wonder if she hates my name.

■

*They never remember the victims' names. I've lost mine. My story is so old that to them, I'm faceless, nameless, ageless. I'm a shapeless girl, killed by her own mother. It's easier for them to put themselves in the story that way. If they remember nothing about me, it's easier for them to fill in the blanks, to picture their own children face down in the arroyo instead of me. It isn't that they like this, this way of thinking, no, but they crave it anyway.*

*Eleven was the last birthday I had and I'm stuck there. They'll never know my name, but they'll never forget my mother's name. La Llorona, the mother of the unnamed children, roaming the arroyo to snatch new children in the night. They'll be raised to fear her instead of their own mothers.*

*They make no effort to name me.*

■

"Mama?" I say, almost afraid of saying anything.

"Ceanothus, please. I'm busy." She doesn't look up.

I know she's in a mood. She's almost always in a mood, and then when she isn't, she just... isn't. She'll kiss the end of my nose and the top of my head. She'll kiss the sides of my eyes, the squishy corner where tears used to start, back when I was a little kid and I could get away with crying, when crying would make her nice, when crying would make her kiss the sides of my eyes. If I cried right now she would not want to look at me. "Pull it together," she would say.

Her hands stop their work, but just for a second. She's slicing the stems off chiles, shaking out the seeds into a bowl. She lifts her hand to wipe her face but stops herself in time.

"What is it?" she finally asks, and sets down the paring knife. She smiles, her mouth closed, her eyes extra crinkly.

"Can I go out?"

"I'm making dinner." The smile and the extra crinkle is gone.

"I'll be back in time," I say and I try to hold the protest out of my voice.

"Fine. Just stay away from the river."

■

*You are just like me. I've watched you the most. You are when I feel the closest to my own mother.*

■

Our house is small with hardly any land. But the land that we do not have, nobody else has either. My mother says it's for everyone as much as it's for no-one. She'll let me use her father's old opera glasses, as long as I'm careful with them, and as long as I don't light anything on fire, so I stuff them into my pocket. I climb over the downed chain-link fence at the end of our backyard, and I'm in the no-man's land. It's protected by the government but watched by nobody. Sometimes I feel like that too.

It only takes a few minutes before I can see the river, the arroyo, grey and slow.

■

*When you were a baby, very small and useless, she would sing to you, satisfied that you'd be too young remember the sad song of the Weeping Woman:*

*Don't think that because I sing, Llorona,*

*My heart is warm;*

*One sings from pain, Llorona,*

*When weeping can't be done.*

*She'd smile when she gazed at you, but her face changed when she looked away. She was a good mother, even though she was alone. She was my favorite of the mothers just like you were my favorite of the babies. It's because you were just like us.*

■

I can hear my mother's shouts but I think it's still okay to ignore them. She's only saying things like, Dinner is almost ready! and, Start heading home! Her voice is small and distant, but I'm close enough to smell the soup on the stove, the warm onion, the sharp chile. I see movement across the river out of the corner of my eye, and at the same time, I hear a noise on this side of the river. Rustling, an animal. Beneath my feet, I see a small horned lizard waddling slowly beneath the scrub, but it isn't making a sound. I look back up to the other side of the river and wriggle the opera glasses out of my back pocket. My shorts are old, too tight, too small.

"Ceanothus!" I hear. "Get home now!"

It's time. It's no longer okay to ignore her but then it all happens so fast. Surely it isn't just in my head: I see something across the river again, in the empty land, vast no-man's land for miles and miles. I snap open the mint green case, and as I lift the opera glasses out and bring them to my face, I hear that rustling again by my feet. I pivot, I lose my balance, I lose my grip. I hear a clink, a thud, and a small splash. The glasses.

■

*I didn't mean it. It was an accident.*

■

I run. Fast. I hurdle over boulders, over low yucca, over downed tree trunks, never slowing down. I fall twice. Once, I brace with my hands, and I'm fine. Twice, my face hits the cold ground and I feel my teeth cut against the bumpy inside of my cheek. I taste blood in my mouth.

"Mama!" I shout, my fear not quite catching up with me yet. I just want her help. "Mama!!"

"Ceanothus?!" she calls, rushing towards the downed chain-link fence in our yard. It's angry-worry I see on her face and that snaps me out of my own rush and no, no, this is not excitement. No, she will not be on my side. No, we will not be a team, mother and son united to find a lost object.

"Ceanothus!" she cries, wronged. "You're hurt!"

She's looking at my shirt, reaching out for it, for the drops of blood and spit. I touch my mouth, and it's sore but it's all there.

"I'm fine, Mama," I say. I suddenly wish I hadn't come running. I wish I hadn't fallen on the way. I wish I'd waited. One day, days, weeks, months, maybe even years later.

She'd ask me "Hey, do you happen to know where my father's opera glasses are?" And I'd shrug. I'd not really answer and she'd move on, frustrated at her own untidiness. But it's too late. I'm holding the empty case in my hand.

"It's broken," she says.

"I fell holding it."

"Ceanothus?" she says quietly, too quiet for the wildness of her eyes. "It's empty."

■

*Don't worry. I'm guarding them. I'm afraid too. I'm always afraid now. I didn't know until it was too late that mothers are something to be afraid of. My mother is here too, on the other side, and it's not your object that she wants.*

■

We're not running. She is striding ahead of me, her thick black hair, still in yesterday's braid, flicking from side to side. I skulk behind.

"Get up here," she hisses. "Hurry up."

I move closer. Not too close.

"Where are they?"

"Um," I say, and I glance towards the river. I hate myself for glancing towards the river.

"Ceanothus. I *said*. I said not to go near the river. You know how dangerous it is! You could have drowned!"

"I didn't, Mama."

"You could have drowned!! Oh god. You never listen," she says, and she's marching towards the river bank.

The arroyo is always so pretty at dinner time, golden and blinding. Gnats hang in the air in front of me, and I breathe one in, gagging.

"I didn't drown, Mama," I say but she's already talking over me.

"I can't trust you! I can't trust you with things or with listening! I need some help from you, here, C. I give up. I don't know what to do with you!"

"I didn't go in the river," I say and this time she heard me.

"I didn't ask you not to go in the river," she says through her teeth. "I asked you to stay AWAY."

"It was here," I say.

She stares at me, her hands on her hips. "What?"

"Here," I say, and then I see a new glint of light, metal and glass, right there, inches from the shore. "There!!"

I push past her but she doesn't understand. She doesn't understand that I see the opera glasses. I'm just trying to help. I'm just trying to get her father's things back for her. Her father, who she hasn't spoken to in eleven years. Her father, who I haven't seen since I was just a few months old. Her father, the grower of *ceanothus*, grandfather of nobody. I'm just trying to get the opera glasses from the river.

But she grabs at me. She grasps a handful of my shirt on her way down, because when I push past her, I push her hard enough to knock her off-balance.

"The glasses!" I shout, and I power forward. I don't want to think about anything except glass and metal and river.

She's up, and she is plowing towards me.

"Stop it right now, young man."

Maybe I should have listened to her. I bend at the waist, my fingertips stretching towards the glasses. They're not far out, pushed against a protruding rock. It's very rocky here. I can reach them. Maybe I can take a few steps in. The river is slower than usual. I know I can reach! But my mother reaches me first.

She falls. Or maybe she lunges.

The majority of her weight hits me on the back of my thighs and I fly a little, a weird mix of weightlessness and heavy, heavy gravity. My head hits first, something hard and sharp, and then—

■

*I'm underwater too. You are just like me. You are when I feel the closest to my mother. I can hear you try to scream. And then I just hear your mother, somewhere between a whisper and a shout,*

*"No, no no no. Ceanothus, no."*

# GUERILLA

## Pepe Rojo

*"Rooted in conspiracy theory and Anti-American sentiment, the Chupacabra is a contradictory and bizarre amalgamation of vampiric monster, folk myth, and chameleon. It is a shapeshifter, changing its appearance and characteristics according to the time and place it is seen, and according to the beliefs and expectations of those who see it."*

- Benjamin Radorf, *Tracking the Chupacabra*

It's ideological, I say. Get the girls pregnant, kill the little boys, say some of mine. I'm not much for tactics; as far as I'm concerned, kill the little girls, get the little boys pregnant. Either way, we'll get there.

Human smell. White human smell. The newcomers. Tender meat. Tender years. My kind of prey. We're moving up from goats. It's not just that I enjoy meat, human or caprine; let's call it heritage responsibility. You see, we were here before everyone else arrived. We had pacts. We had blood contracts. We will be here after everyone leaves. This is geopolitical. I'm just tipping the scales.

The little female is playing alone. Good. That makes it easier. The dry wind is always sour. She is alone. Approach against the wind. Think the long time. Think geological.

But also think revenge. We've learned their language to better camouflage ourselves. We have been turned into clowns by their media. A caricature, a freakish creature. What should have been a slow revolution, a long take-over, was turned into a diversion, a caricature, a media event. We were détourned. They didn't even grant us the elegance of a metaphor. Degraded. But we are growing. We are feeding. Our time is long. After the humiliation of being thrown into the monster freak show, we've learned to hide ourselves behind their pop culture. Guerrilla pop camouflage.

It is getting late for small humans. Soon, her parents will call her in. She knows, and tries to make the most of her time by straying away from her house. Good for me. Good for the cause.

Genetically. Psychologically. Semiotically. Geographically. We are just helping them get over their own fast-approaching tipping point. The desert we roam is vast. Timeless.

She notices something and raises her head, but I am the land and she can not see me. Entranced by an idiotical chant she learned from a screen, she returns to play. I make my move. I time my time. I jump over her. Our gazes cross. In that timeless moment, she knows this is the right thing to happen, she knows she is the invader and her adrenaline fills the air. My bite steals the scream from her throat. The blood tastes of guilt.

Her body's still shaking while I tear up some chunks of meat, and then I leave.

We are growing. We are patient. We'll get there. Our time is long.

# TAKE THE TIME TO UNDERSTAND YOURSELVES

## Jimmy Callaway

*"Either way, it is difficult not to wonder why aliens — who
seem so insistent on warning us to change our ways before
it's too late — consistently choose ordinary people of little
or no political, social or economic influence upon which to
impart their dire warnings. It would seem as if a world leader,
an entrepreneur billionaire like Bill Gates or even Brad Pitt
would be a better bet to get their message across. Still, who
are we to question the motives of giant, blue space brains?"*

- Rob Morphy, *American Monsters*

"Ah, man," John said. His eyes were too tired to be angry. "Today. You picked today
to come outside." And then the atomic wave rushed over us and burned our skin off,
burned our hair off, burned us off the face of the earth.

That morning, I convinced John we should leave the bomb shelter and go get some ice
cream.

John fetched a sigh and looked forlornly at the last couple cans of hash we had left.
"Yeah, might as well."

It was hot out. Very hot. I picked up the newspaper in Mr. Fenton's driveway and saw
that it was August. I dropped the paper before Mr. Fenton accused me of stealing it,
and I realized Mr. Fenton had probably been dead for a while now.

Everything else was pretty much the same, though.

Kind of a drag the world didn't end. I mean, obviously, not a total drag, but still.

I watched John blink his eyes, adjust to natural light. He hadn't shaved for a while,
and in the hot sun his beard at first seemed to recoil and then reach for the light, like
ivy. The gray in his hair was much more pronounced, and I figured mine must look the

same, and my shoulders sagged. John looked the same bummed out that I felt. But also relieved, obviously.

"The Jacksons got rid of their siding," he said.

I turned and looked back at John's house. It looked like it had been haunted for years. Someone had smashed the living room window. A piece of plywood had been hastily nailed over it. The lawn was mowed, though, and the fresh grass smell still hung in the air a bit.

As hot as it was, I soon noticed I was shivering, my teeth clattered in my head. I looked at John and he was rubbing his arms through his robe. "Come on," I said, "Let's go for a walk."

I hadn't had any nightmares since about 1989 or so, and John hadn't woken me up screaming for at least five years. But inevitably, because we're idiots, I guess, we ended up walking down Dapplegray Lane.

There were still no sidewalks. The trees were so green, they hurt my eyes, my lungs. Everyone was inside, out of the heat, and the air hung there like a wet sheet, tensing for an ocean breeze, a car passing by, anything to free us from this moment.

The early '70s. That was the last time either of us had been on this little street. No matter how stupid our pants were, we'd always looked good. A fun night, hanging out with the guys, a few brews. And then we'd been here.

Dapplegray Lane.

At first, it was just, Oh, a couple of brains in the street. No big deal, people litter all the time, even in an upper-class neighborhood.

And then it was, Oh. There are brains in the street.

What always stuck in my mind was the texture. The texture of these brains. Disembodied brains in the middle of the road. That was a concept I never had much trouble with. But the...the texture. It'd sobered me up like a pot of coffee to the face. I could smell the moisture. I could feel the gray, even through the cloud of bluish haze that hung around them like chiffon drapes.

"John," I'd said.

"Yes."

"John. Let's go. Please, let's go."

There was an eye in the middle of one of them. An eye. An eye in a brain. It blinked slowly, and I could feel it, could feel it smearing the sclera clean.

"Yes," John said and drove me home.

I went straight to bed and had my last dreamless sleep for many, many years to come.

After that, I went about my days numbly, eating cereal and going to the beach, all inside a protective suit of flesh I could not feel until the next decade. John, though, he'd had it even worse. When John got home that night after dropping me off, the brains had been waiting for him. At home. At his house.

To be a hundred percent honest here, I was always a little bummed that they clearly didn't want me around. But relieved of course, obviously.
John spent the next handful of years trying to convince people of what we saw, and that the brains—Jesus Christ, the brains from outer space came and abducted John and warned him that Earth was doomed. That we had too much power and it would end up killing us all.

I tried to support him as much as I could, I really did. I went on whatever talk shows and radio programs he dragged me to. I met with whatever reporters or authors John could get to listen. But it was like I was piloting my body and mind through a series of pulleys and levers. The best I could do was nod serenely and say, "That's what we saw, all right."

Nobody seemed to think it was all right.

The brains had taken John to a spaceship where they told John that total nuclear war would break out in 1982. They even showed him footage of it somehow. To be one hundred percent honest, I didn't buy that at first. But then Governor Reagan became President Reagan. And so, in late 1979, I began helping John build his bomb shelter in earnest.

We kept a TV and radio, and 1982 came and went and it seemed to me the worst thing to happen was Vic Morrow getting killed. By Christmas that year, I tried to leave but John stopped me, said that we should hang out just to be safe. "Just till January, man, just to be sure."

That night, the brains came to me in my sleep. "Take your time," they said, "Take the time to understand yourselves."

John woke me up with his screaming. Neither of us mentioned leaving again. Until today.

Why today? Why did I pick today? Did I understand myself? Or was I just, y'know. Bored.

We walked quickly off Dapplegray Lane, our bathrobes blowing behind us, our asses puckered and trying to get ahead of us. We cut through Dapplegray Park where Palos Verdes Drive East meets Palos Verdes Drive North. We were pretty sure there used to be an ice cream place up on Western, but it would be kind of a hike.

Even on Palos Verdes Drive, there was no traffic. I was trying to decide if this is weird or not, if maybe they'd cut down on traffic here in the 21st century, when the air raid sirens started. We could hear them all, it seemed, from Long Beach to Hermosa. John grabbed me by my robe. Spittle flew from his lips, but his eyes were more tired than angry. Like he was going through the motions.

"Ah, man!" he said, "Today! You had to pick today to come outside!" And then a flash of light behind me and I watched John's retinas burn out.

And I said, "Today's as good a day as any other. We could have been at the beach this whole time, we could have been going to school or working as firemen. We've been underground for over thirty years, and we don't have any idea what's going on. We're just going to die like everyone else now." But he didn't hear me because first the incredible bang and then the heat blast rolled over Los Angeles from who knows how many atomic bombs dropped on it.

Our molecules, our atoms disbanded, defused, went from matter to nothingness, and I was just like, "Huh."

# A Mythical Terrestrial Cetacean as Deus Ex Machina Or, Dave McCormick Finally Gets What's Coming To Him

## Matt Lewis

*"In the mountains of Colorado, where in summer the woods are becoming infested with tourists, much uneasiness has been caused by the presence of the Slide Rock Bolter. This frightful animal lives only in the steepest mountain country. The Bolter comes down like a toboggan, scooping in its victim as it goes, its own impetus carrying it up the next slope, where it again slaps its tail over the ridge and waits."*

- William T. Cox, *Fearsome Animals of the Lumberwoods*

The last thing he remembered was throwing up in the Del Taco just outside of Denver and getting dragged out by the neck while employees shouted at him in Spanish.

"Rob, you fuckin' ruined that place. It was everywhere," said Damien, the black blocks of his sunglasses reflecting in the rearview mirror. "Just fuckin' ruined it."

Kingston was still giggling about the whole thing. "Holy shit, son. Hooooooollly shit." He started rolling a spliff on a magazine in his lap.

Bile still burned at the back of Rob's throat. He was in a fetal position in the backseat of the Astrovan. The seat smelled like a moldy basement's ass.

Rob's head pounded with the ache of Jameson and regret. But it wasn't just blind pain; hangovers were the only moments that ever gave him enough pause for a reflection on his life. He was forty-five years old and still playing in a punk band. Drinking every night with kids half his age. Barely scraping by. *But that's okay,* he thought. *This is what I wanted. This is the life I've chosen.*

■

Ever since his first high school punk band, the Almond Brothers, Rob had been in love with playing bass. He jumped around from band to band, playing with some real shit shows like The Fuckbutts, Chima & the Losers, the Crock Pot Avengers—he even sat in with Genetically Modified Orgasms for a few nights. Sometimes he felt like quitting, but he thought of himself as too stubborn and, to be totally honest, too scared to change. The thought of a cheesy sales job made him want to jump into moving traffic.

Getting by wasn't too bad—punk houses & squats had been the best places to crash. He got to know a network of people and found he could travel all over the country with enough connections. That's how he met the current bandmates. Damien, a white trash kid straight out of a Nevada trailer park, played riffs that hit like a lightning bolt. And Kingston, who seemed like the most mellow Rasta black kid Rob had ever met, screamed into a microphone like he was possessed. *Unbelievable.* He even loved the band name: These Shitkickin' Boots. A little green around the edges, but Rob thought they had all the makings of a powerhouse band. Or they would have been, if the drummer, Kip, hadn't split with some girl in Denver. So here they were, heading toward a gig in Salt Lake City in a van filled with drums and no one to play them.

"So who's gonna drum for us tomorrow night?" Rob asked Kingston. He lit the spliff, inhaled deeply, and blew a plume of smoke out the window.

"Damien's got it taken care of," Kingston said.

"Oh really?" Rob said. "Who'd you get, Damien? You know some Mormons who can drum?"

Damien shifted uncomfortably in the driver's seat. "I got someone here. We'll be picking him up pretty soon."

"Yeah? Who?"

"Dave McCor —"

"—No."

"Yes, man, Dave's the only guy available!"

"Then I'm not fucking playing!" Rob yelled at him. His hoarse throat stung from the strain.

Damien pulled the van to the side of the road. He lowered his sunglasses and Rob saw his eyes for the first time that day. They were bloodshot and worried.

"Dude. I'm not any happier about it than you are. But he's all we can get right now. I swear he'll be cool, okay?"

"Whatever, dude. It's your rodeo." Rob crouched back into the smelly folds of the seat. "But let the record show that I told you right here and now: Dave McCormick is a fucking liability."

"So, who are we talking about?" Kingston asked.

Rob took it upon himself to answer. "The sketchiest asshole drummer this side of the Mississippi. I've played gigs with him half a dozen times and his craziness ruined every single one of them. Last time I saw him, he was getting arrested in Boulder for pulling a knife on Sara, his girlfriend at the time."

"Holy shit!" Kingston's eyes went wide. "Why'd he do that?"

"They had this dog named Bella—well, it was Sara's dog, but he said it belonged to him. They got in an argument and she called the cops. I heard she took off to Canada and sent the dog to live with someone else.
No wonder he's still in Colorado—he's probably on probation or something and couldn't leave the state."

"Well, damn. Who's stupid enough to keep giving this guy a chance?" Kingston wondered.

"Us, apparently," Rob said. The van went quiet as they pulled into the parking lot of a roadside Subway shop, just as the sun slid from its peak into late afternoon.

"Dave says he's in Subway right now," Damien said, checking the texts on his phone. "Thank GOD. Didn't even get to eat breakfast 'cause of puker over here." Damien gestured toward Rob. Kingston chuckled quietly.

"Whatever. If you think that shit was bad, I don't think you're ready to deal with Dave."

Damien laughed and stepped out of the van. Rob decided to get out too, even though he felt like his head would crack open. He needed some water and didn't think there was any liquid left in his body to puke out. They stepped into the air-conditioned Subway and immediately heard loud, annoyed voices. Dave was standing in front of the cash register and shoving a sub into his mouth as fast as he could. *Here we go,* Rob thought.

"Sir!" a short girl in a ponytail behind the counter said. "Your credit card isn't going through. Please stop eating that!"

"Naw, dawg," Dave said, spitting crumbs. "Try swiping it UP. You didn't swipe it UP, that's why it's not working."

"Try it, Jodie," a man standing behind the girl said. From his age and uniform, Rob assumed he was the manager. He looked paunchy and tired.

"It's still not working. Sir, PLEASE." She held her hands up.

"It's not? Wow, damn. Yeah, that's some shit," Dave said, shoving the last bit of sub into his mouth. Then he grabbed the card out of her hand and walked toward the door, like it was the most natural exchange in the world.

The poor girl and her manager just stood there, flabbergasted for a minute. The she yelled at the top of her lungs "Hey, ASSHOLE!"

"Jodie, please!" her manager grabbed her arm and whispered harshly in her ear. A scary-looking biker gang poked their heads up over the booths to see what's going on.

Dave looked at Rob like he just woke up. "Don't know what their problem is, man," he said. "So, we dippin' or what?"

"But we haven't eaten yet."

Some of the bikers had walked over to the counter and were talking with the manager, who was pointing at Dave.  Rob could see them get the death glare from all around the room.

"Damien," Rob whispered, grabbing his arm. "Thanks to your friend here, if we stay we're gonna get stomped by these burly-ass bikers for fuckin' over their favorite restaurant. What would you rather do, go hungry or lose some teeth?"

Damien got the gist. "Yeah, alright," he said. "Let's go."

"C'mon, Dave." Rob said.

"Uh, sure, yeah," Dave said, who eyed Rob with suspicion. "Sorry, what's your name, dude? I don't think we've met before."

*That moving traffic is starting to sound better and better*, Rob thought.

■

Back on the road to Salt Lake, Rob tried to refresh Dave's memory. "It's Rob, Dave. R-O-B. From Bakersfield, remember? We played together at the Tower in San Diego and you almost burned it down?"
Dave just shook his head and started out the window. "Sorry, bro. Not ringin' a bell."

"How about Chicago? You were sitting in with the Bill Men, but instead of playing you snuck off into the parking lot and tried to steal the bouncer's car?" Rob's voice started to rise in annoyance. "You took off and I broke my nose trying to pull that bouncer off of their guitarist? Did you hear about that part?"

"Hm, nope. No idea."

"Jesus Christ," Rob moaned and collapsed back on the seat.

"You're lucky I was available, dawg," he said, lighting up a cigarette in the back of the van. "I got a lot of shit going on. Lots of important gigs, job offers, you know. These drums, too, these look like pieces of shit. Not what I'm used to playing on at ALL, dawg. Don't you guys have money? Or do you just not care about how you sound? Fuckin' AMATEUR, dude."

Damien ignored him. Kingston stared blankly at the roadside signs. He said out loud, "San Juan National Forest, next..."

Dave bolted up. "San Juan National Forest?!? Pull over! We gotta go there dawg, we gotta go!" He started rapping on the window with his knuckles and jiggled the door handle.

"Knock it off, you fuckhead! What is wrong with you?" Rob snapped at him.

Dave had a bug-eyed, crazy look on his face. "That's where my girl took my dog, dude. She took my dog to her friend Parker who lives on a campground near San Juan National Forest. We need to go get my Bella!"

"Dude, that place is like, six miles in the other direction. Forget it."

"Then I won't play," Dave said defiantly. "I need my dog, man. We need to go get Bella. Either that or I'll hop out right now!"

Damien looked at his iphone map and sighed deeply. "Okay, man. As long as you know where to go, it shouldn't be too out of the way."

Rob moaned in protest, but didn't feel like arguing. He fell into the seat and tried to sleep.

■

When Rob woke up, the sun was just starting to set. The green landscape was tinted orange and yellow by the fading light. He got up and saw that they were parked in the lot of souvenir shop made to look like a cabin. Damien rolled open the van door.

"So, update," he said, frowning. "Dave sent us a couple of miles in the wrong direction."

"Big fuckin' surprise there."

"I pulled off here to get directions, but as soon as we parked, Dave went running down this trailhead. He said it would lead to the campground where that guy lives. The guy in the store says we can take this road in the van and get there in an hour."

Rob glared at him like a gargoyle.

"Dude, I KNOW. But we're already all the way out here, so..."

Kingston ran out toward them from the shop, holding something in his hands and laughing like a maniac. "Check this shit out! This shit is COMEDY!"

He shoved a postcard into Rob's hand. It was an old-timey drawing of a huge whale with sharp teeth sliding down a mountain, toward some fleeing people. 'The Slide-Rock Bolter', the caption said. 'Legend has it that in the 18th century, lumberjacks discovered this monster would slide down mountain-sides and devour everything in its path...'

"Fuck, King, this is just some tourist trap shit. Don't waste your money."

Damien looked at the sunset. "It's gonna be dark soon. We should get over to that campground if we're gonna find him."

"Yeah!" Kingston said, talking in a spooky voice and waving his hands around. "We have to find him before daaaaaaaaaarrrrk, before the Slide Rock Bolter GETS YOU!"

■

They got to the campground at dusk and found Parker pretty easily. He was sitting in front of his tent and nursing a black eye. Apparently, Dave had showed up, saw Parker with Bella the dog and attacked him.

"It was fucked up, man. Sara didn't want him to get near the poor thing. Bella recognized him and ran off, so he started chasing her into the woods. He's a fucking psychopath."

"Yeah, we know," Rob said, giving Damien the stink-eye. "Did you see which way he went?"

Parker pointed toward a dark trail entrance where the treeline ended. Some yellow 'caution' tape was strung between the trees. "They both ran off that way. It takes you toward the base of some of the mountains. They closed it last week because of rock slides."

"Perfect," Rob said. "Because there's no one I'd rather risk my life for."
He walked toward the trailhead. "King, you stay with the van. Damien, you're with me. Let's find this idiot and get back on the road."

Damien hesitated. "What about the rock slides? Isn't it dangerous?"

Rob walked right up into Damien's face. "Listen. It was your idea to recruit this ass-hole. All day I've had to listen to him bitch and moan and hear you make excuses for him. You said you were gonna take responsibility for his shit, right? Well..." He dug some flashlights out of the van and threw them to him. "Get your scrawny ass on that trail and man up."

About twenty minutes into the walk, the flashlights were the only light they had. The woods hummed with crickets and God knew what else. They were just about ready to give up when they heard Dave's voice just past a bend in the trail.

"Bella! Bella! Where are you, dawg? Bella! BELLA!"

"Dave!" Rob yelled out. "Forget about the dog! We're here to lead you out!"

There was a silence.

"Who is that?"

"It's us! Rob and Damien! We're here to get you back to the van!"

A short pause. "Wait, *who?* Who's Rob?!?"

*Seriously?* Rob turned around and started to walk back.

"Wait, dude!" Damien said. "He's just fuckin' around. I'm sure—"

Before he could finish, the forest floor started to rumble. Pine needles vibrated on the ground and huge flocks of birds screeched and erupted in flight overhead. Rob started to hear trees snapping like cracks of lightning, getting closer and closer every second.

"Rock slide!" Rob yelled. "Everybody—"

But something erupted through the treeline, and it was no rock slide. They saw a huge gray leviathan smash through the trail just ahead, with a gaping mouth full of sharp yellow teeth. Rob dove for cover from the falling branches. Then, quickly as it had appeared, the thing had vanished.

When they were sure it was safe, they crept up past the bend in the trail where they heard Dave's voice. It was completely devastated. Where the trail had been, there was a huge chunk cut out of the earth that separated one side from the other by about a hundred feet. Forty foot trees were smashed into the ground like toothpicks.

There was a huge path that had been cleared from the top of the mountain, then down past the trail and far off into the forest. Rob looked at Damien. He was white as a sheet.

"Wh-wha-what...what? Rob...was that...the thing?"

Rob sighed and shook his head. "Call it a rock slide, call it a monster, call it whatever you want. I'm gonna call it karma and wash my hands of this shit."

They walked back to the campsite in silence. Even the crickets seemed to have muted their noise. When they got there, King was sitting in the van, holding a German Shepard that was panting heavily. Rob recognized the dog. It was Bella.

"Look who I found!" Kingston said, smiling. "Hey, where's Dave? You guys couldn't find him?"

Rob and Damien looked at each other. Damien raised his eyebrows and started to speak, but Rob cut him off.

"Nope. Didn't find him," Rob said. "He could be anywhere, I guess. He'll probably come back to the campsite eventually."

Kingston nodded. "Fine with that. We should take off before he gets back. That dude was unstable. I don't wanna drive around with a nutcase like him."

Damien looked at Rob and understood the story. He nodded in agreement.

"Yeah, we should get back on the road. We can always find another drummer in Salt Lake."

Rob walked Bella back to the campsite. He told Parker that they didn't find Dave, but he didn't care. He was just glad they brought the dog back.

"I told some friends nearby to keep an eye out for Dave," Parker told him. "That fucker's gonna have some problems if he tries that shit again."

Rob just nodded. "Yeah, I expect he will." He walked back to the van and saw Damien & Kingston back in their seats. He got in the backseat and they drove out of the campground and back toward the highway.

As they drove away, Kingston pointed at the mountainside where the thing had slid down. There was a great brown gash in the side of the rock-encrusted hill.

"Dude. Did you guys HEAR that huge rock slide while you were in there? For a second I thought y'all got caught up in it!" He paused and his face turned serious. "Hey, you don't think Dave was—"

"Nah," Damien said. "We could still hear Dave yelling for the dog after that. He just wasn't listening to us when we called him."

Kingston shook his head. "Damn, that dude's dumb. That shit is no joke. But after all that bullshit that Rob said he pulled, maybe he would have had it comin'!"

Rob collapsed into the folds of the backseat.

"Yeah," he said. "Maybe he did."

# THE MIDWEST

NEBRASKA ■ PHANTOM KANGAROOS
## Between a Gas Station and the American Frontier

OHIO ◆ THE LOVELAND FROG
## Punctuated Equilibrium

NORTH DAKOTA ■ THE THUNDERBIRD
## Wakíyą

MINNESOTA ◆ THE WENDIGO
## River Run

MACLEAN 2014

# SOMEWHERE BETWEEN A GAS STATION AND THE AMERICAN FRONTIER

## Keith McCleary

*"A prime example of an animal turning up where it shouldn't, Phantom Kangaroos have been seen on numerous occasions across the continent – with most reports occurring in the Midwest. In instances of Phantom Kangaroo sightings, the first inclination is to check with local zoos that usually report no animals missing. To make matters stranger, the kangaroos do not appear normal. They seem overly aggressive and have fierce teeth."*

- Scott Francis, *Monster Spotter's Guide to North America*

I told my father that life had become a road leading into nothing, and each stop alongside it was the same. I told him life was a flat plain leading to a gray horizon, but the horizon was lost in fog.

"You know," he said, "everyone turns 30. This isn't something invented for you."

"Did everyone lose *all three* of their jobs when they turned 30?" I asked him. "Did everyone's girlfriend move to Guam three weeks before they turned 30? Did everyone run out of money and have to move home with their parents for Christmas after they turned 30? Is everyone sitting on their parents' couch at 3am crying to their father? Did everyone's girlfriend dump them for a dude who's 42? Is everyone still taking care of their girlfriend's cat?"

Grace meowed from my lap, hearing the word "cat" and assuming she would be fed.

From the basement, my mother's cat whined. We'd been keeping the two animals in separate corners of the house since I'd brought Grace home.

My father might have fallen asleep while I was talking. I cried some more, and blew my nose. In the dark I felt him jump. He sat up next to me.

"It's self-actualization, Dad," I said. "I'm at the mercy of my sadness. It's like I'm living at the edge of an abyss attempting not to fall in, but I'm being consumed."

The word consumed became something like "con-su-hu-hu-huaah," and I cried some more. My dad patted my back a few times and fell asleep with his hand on my shoulder. I sighed and the sigh was so wracked with heartache that the couch shook. My dad woke again.

Grace meowed, wondering about the feeding.

"We need to self-actualize that cat on out of here," my father said.

It was never planned that I would keep the cat. The problem was getting rid of her. She hadn't flown to Guam because the vet said she had a bad heart and couldn't fly. None of my friends in Brooklyn had wanted her; they were already overloaded with abandoned cats. My ex-girlfriend's family lived in Nebraska. They offered to take Grace. They even suggested we each drive halfway, and meet up south of Chicago to do a transfer.

I hadn't driven a car in ten years, but my father was a highway warrior. He'd shown up at my door in Brooklyn after my ex had gone, helped throw away the takeout containers and layers of Kleenexes across my floor, loaded up as many boxes of clothes and books as his pickup would hold, and drove them six hours to our house in upstate New York.  Then he'd driven six hours back in same day to get me and Grace. He led me through the move like I was an invalid, and waited in the truck while I turned over the keys to my Hasidic landlord.

On that drive upstate we'd stopped once, at the Mediterranean Diner and Pizzeria off the I-80, north of the Hope Township. My father made do with a hamburger while I tried the spaghetti. He paid for both.

"Thanks for driving all this way," I'd said. "I know this is a little crazy."

"It's fine," he said. "I'm just glad the library got some new Stephanie Plum novels on tape."

"And I can drive you to Chicago too," he said that night as we pulled into our driveway and my mother came out to greet us. "I never got the chance to meet her folks anyway."

"You're so weird," I said. "But thanks."

It took several weeks to find a time that would work for both our families. The night before we left, I couldn't sleep. By 3am, I'd woken my father up to sit with me while I cried. At 6am, we both gave up on sleeping, and decided to pack the truck.

"Should we be eating this many donuts?" I asked a half hour later. We'd just left the last gas station out of town. I had three crullers stuffed in my mouth at once.

"We just won't tell your mother," my father said. He was on his second cup of coffee, which he shouldn't have been drinking because of his heart.

"We won't tell her about this either," he said.

As we drove through town the sun rose. The snow was heaped on every surface, covering house and hedgerow. The occasional delivery truck passed us on the road to the highway, its headlights glowing yellow against the white.

"The cocoa's good," I said. Next to me on the seat Grace yowled from her carrier, wondering if she would ever be fed again.

We drove north to hit I-90, which would carry us all the way from Buffalo through Indiana, where other highways led on toward Chicago—and all the way to Lincoln, if we wanted. We listened to Stephanie Plum trade
witty banter with her detective boyfriend. It was like *Murder She Wrote* with drinking and guns.

"You paying attention to this?" my father asked.

"I could listen to something else," I said.

"You remember when I used to tell you about Johan Shedlebauer?" my dad asked.

"That's not really what I meant," I said.

My dad's ability to improvise bedroom stories when I was a child had needed an outlet as I got older. During fourth grade, he got stuck on the unusual last name of my history teacher. While Mr. Schedlebauer took us through the basics of post-colonial America by day, my father spun tales of the Schedlebauer family's contributions to the Revolutionary War and the westward expansion over dinner each evening. The star of his stories was Johan Schedlebauer, a war hero and adventurer who was as immortal as my father needed him to be, and who had found himself, as required, in the midst of each chapter of my history lessons.

"Too bad," my father said now, as we drove west. "I got this great story about how Johan Schedlebauer helped take down Al Capone."

We'd decided to meet my ex's parents in Gary, Indiana. By eleven o'clock, my father was singing *Music Man* tunes as we pulled into a Rally's Hamburger joint in downtown Gary, two blocks from the interstate.

"Her parents texted," I said, checking my phone as we ate. "They got a late start. Said we could wait for them here, or meet them further west."

"We don't have anywhere else to be," my father said, and ordered a coffee for the road.

It's when Illinois turns into Iowa that the world turns weird, and gets weirder all the way to the Rockies. Not the same kind of weird the entire route—but wilder and woolier, like Johan Schedlebauer and his fellow explorers ran out of energy for taming the land once they saw how it flattened and emptied, as the hills became plains and the forests turned to scrubs. The clock on my father's truck dashboard kept running numbers to indicate the crawl into early afternoon, but past our windows the world seemed to slow.

"This reminds me of when we did that drive to Northern Georgia," my father said.

In my early twenties I thought I had a career ahead of me in film. I was shooting industrials around New York, started contacting zoos in search of something wilder. Smaller jobs led me to get hired on a shoot for an animal conservation facility outside Atlanta, south of the Chattahoochee National Forest. Their specialty was kangaroos.

It was a long trip for a handful of art students accustomed to city living. My father had just retired, and offered to drive our van. We spent four days chasing giant, loping marsupials across the Georgia mountains. I still have a photo of him petting a joey. It was quite a time.

"Wow," I said now, as we passed signs for Des Moines. "I forgot about that. Have you been driving me across the country my whole life?"

"Well, I might have," my father said. "Have you heard from her parents yet?"

I checked my phone. "They say they're stuck," I said.

"Stuck?" he said. "Stuck on what? There's no one out here."

He gestured to the road. The deep snows of the Northeast were gone, but an icy crust covered everything, and grayed the horizon and the sky into a blur. For awhile we'd seen a car or two on the highway opposite, but now we were driving alone.

"Maybe there's a storm," my father said, and clicked on the radio. He spun the dial to a sequences of hisses and clicks. "Huh," he said.

We pulled into the next gas station. "I need some coffee," he said, and we went inside.

The lights were off in the station, and it was quiet. At the counter, a teenage girl and boy were sitting near the registers and watching the highway. My dad poured himself some coffee from the dregs of a lukewarm-looking pot.

The girl behind the counter looked at me as I played with my phone. "Is yours working?" she asked. "Mine's been dead all morning."

"There's a blackout, stupid," the boy said.

"Phones don't blackout, stupid," said the girl. "They're on satellites."

"Maybe a satellite fell," the boy said. "Because of the blackout."

"Oh my God. I apologize for him. I think he was homeschooled," the girl said as she used a calculator to ring us up.

"There's a blackout?" I asked.

"All the way to Lincoln," the boy said.

"When did we hit Nebraska?" I asked my father. "Weren't we in Iowa?"

"Well, I don't know," my father said.

Grace mewled from her carrier when we got back to the truck. I put a leash on her and let her pee outside. She tried scratching at the frozen pavement to cover it.

As I hopped into the car with Grace my father started the engine. He put the truck into gear and crept toward the highway, then shouted, "Holy crap!"
I had a moment to look at him, follow his eyes, squeeze Grace so hard she scratched me, then turn to the road as a giant metal lump crashed to the asphalt.

"What the hell was that?" I asked.

"Well I don't know," my father said. We parked the truck and got out, as the boy and girl from the station ran out toward us. We stood over the foreign object for a moment. Then the boy shouted.

"Ha!" he turned to the girl. "In your face! Crashed satellite! I told you! *Just like I said!*"

We helped the kids push the metal and detritus off the highway, and with nothing else to do, we got back on the road.

"Maybe we'll just drive all the way there if we don't hear from her parents soon," my father said.

"Yeah," I said. "My phone's dead anyway." I paused. "But really, a satellite falling? That doesn't make sense."

"It sure doesn't," my father said. "What did you call it? This morning before we left, you said something funny."

"When I was crying and in despair? I don't think I was being funny," I said.

"Sure," my father said. "You talked about life being a plain or something —well, like this." He gestured at the empty road. "What did you call it? Self-something."

"Self-actualization," I said.

"Right!" my father said. He laughed. "Maybe that kid self-actualized a satellite, and that's what made it fall."

"You're so weird," I said. "That's literally the weirdest thing." We drove again for awhile.

"Johan Schedlebauer and his men were lost in a fog like this once," my father said. "They were exploring the great plains, just like we are."

"Is this before or after Al Capone?" I asked.

"Before," my father said. "He was younger. He'd thought he'd got his life together, but then he got a 'Dear John' letter from Mrs. Schedlebauer. You know what that means?"

"Yes Dad," I said.

"Okay. But in this case it was a 'Dear *Johan*' letter."

"You're killing me," I said.

"Okay," my father said. "So Johan decided to take one last job on the frontier. He got hired to transport some cattle. He got his men together and they went west. It was fine until a storm rolled in. They lost their cattle and they were wandering in the mist for days."

I watched the fog roll in outside our window. "Okay," I said. "So then what?"

"Funniest thing," he said. "Because decades earlier, Johan's father, who was also Johan, had been traveling through the frontier with a circus. And that circus had also gotten lost in a storm. The same storm. This 100-year storm out in the plains of Nebraska. And like with Johan Jr, all of Johan Sr's circus animals got loose. And the only ones to survive out there all those years—"

"Oh brother—" I said.

"—was a mob of wild kangaroos. A mob, right? Isn't that what they're called?"

"Christ," I said. "Yeah, Dad. It's a mob."

"So Johan Jr found those kangaroos, and luckily for Johan, his father had taught him to speak with animals. So Johan and his men were able to follow the kangaroos back out."

"Terrible," I said. "So where are these kangaroos now? I mean, those have got be some tough kangaroos. How come we don't see them in Nebraska anymore?"

"Well, they were *phantom* kangaroos," my father said. "You wouldn't want to see them anyway. Kinda scary from living in the plains so long. Look, here's another station. I have to pee."

We pulled off the road again in front of a gas station identical to the last one we'd seen. The world around us was a wall of grey. Another car was parked in front. We pulled up next to it and got out.

"That car looks familiar," I said.

"Holy crap!" a woman's voice said, behind us. We turned to see my ex-girlfriend's mother come out of the station, carrying coffee. She walked up to us, and hugged me.

"Thank God!" she said. "I'm so sorry about this. Thanks for bringing Grace!"

"It's okay," I said. My father and my ex's mother shook hands.

"You know it's like I've been driving for hours," she said. "This storm rolled in and the whole state shut down. I swear, I haven't been able to make it to the border. I can't even see where I'm going. I just gave up and pulled over, and here you are."

"I guess so," I said.

"I'm going to pee," my father said, and went inside. My ex's mother nuzzled Grace, and Grace swatted her.

"Poor baby," she said. Then she looked at me. "You're both poor babies."

"Yeah," I said.

My father came out of the gas station with a funny look on his face. "You okay?" I asked him.

"I don't know," he said. "Those kids at the counter were awful familiar."

I looked past him. Inside were two kids at the register. They did look familiar. I turned to look past the pumps, and saw a heap of broken satellite on the ground.

"Huh," I said.

As we stood there, I began to hear footsteps on the pavement. Three men came up on us through the fog.

"Ho there," one of them said. He was tall and thin, and his face was rough. All their faces were. They looked sun-browned and strong. Their clothes were fashioned from wool, and they wore vests of animal skins.

"You guys have a breakdown?" my ex's mother said. The men looked at each other skeptically, then back at us.

"We're traveling," the tall man said. "Trying to outpace the storm. We saw your outpost and thought you might have provisions."

"Oh, it's not ours," my father said. "But they're open." The man nodded, and his group walked past us. My father turned to them.

"You guys having any luck getting out of here?" my father said. "I think we're a little lost."

The men looked back at him, and nodded again. "Wait here," the tall man said. They went inside the shop.

"They seem nice," my ex's mother said.
A few minutes later, the men came out again, holding handfuls of Twinkies. They seemed confused. "Provisions are unusual in these parts," the tall man said.

He walked to the road and pulled out an eyeglass—no more than a curl of leather and glass. He peered into the surrounding fog. Then he put it away, cupped his hands to his face and gave a chirruping whistle. It was loud and long. He stamped his foot while he did it—*thump thump, thump.*

Out of the mists, a sequence of shadows began to lope past us. They thudded across the hill on the far side of the highway, out of rhythm. I saw curled backs, arcing legs, straight tails like beacons.

The tall man looked back at us. "They'll lead you out," he said. "We're following them too."

And he and his compatriots disappeared into the fog.

My father and I didn't speak as we drove out of Nebraska, following the mob. The radio fuzzed to life somewhere in western Iowa, warning of storms back the way we'd come. The announcer joked that there was always a storm somewhere in the Great Plains, and sometimes it seemed like it was always the same one.

As the sky cleared, I leaned back in my seat and saw Grace's leash looking at me from the dashboard. I hoped my ex's mother didn't try to let her out without it. Grace had a tendency to run for cover in bad weather.

"I think you can just mail that to her," my father said.

# Punctuated Equilibrium

## Jessica Hilt

*"Loveland is a small, somewhat isolated community, a place where strange stories spread as quickly as the flu. Soon, just about everybody had heard of the two policemen who'd seen a monster out on Twight-wee Road. It was a funny story. Unless you were the two policemen. For them, the notoriety was more than embarrassing. How do you command respect when you believe a frog monster is living in the local river?"*

- James Renner, *It Came From Ohio*

I sensed her in the air. It was not something I inhaled but rather collected through my skin, my eyes, my tongue. It was her secret language, her biology, her song that signaled me. Molecules of her youth racing through my skin, pulling us closer until the moment we met. When I think of her—and how I hate thinking of her—those thoughts come like heat lightning, flashing across my body before I can defend myself with logic. When I think of her, it is not her wide smile, or her thick legs, or her pale, round belly that misleads me into her memory. It is her smell.

Annabel. She had hiked down the hillside to the summer creek, steamy and green, air saturated with cicadas and the aroma of hot mint that choked the summer stream. Pitching herself forward, she slid down the embankment carved out by the creek. It was a shallow rock inlet that surrounded the deepest part of the creek, a black pool. My pool.

Under the water, I twitched at the sight of her, sending ripples through the drowsy current. Tiny fish raced across rocks and into crevices in panicked bursts as they remembered me. The grasses swayed, revealing small insects of their hiding places. Crawdads pushed and clacked over each other and under rocks, sending up puffs of silt. But it was the cicadas that betrayed me in their sudden silence, disturbing the air with a stretch of impossible quiet. The dribble of water over the ridge became the only sound and Annabel froze, scanning the hillside, the swales, before letting her gaze drop to the pool.

The weight of her scrutiny made my heart pound, but I submerged until only my eyes and the dome of my head protruded above the waterline. The mottled green and black of my skin, the texture of bark, would hide me within the pond scum and cattails and if I closed my eyes, I would disappear entirely. But I couldn't bear to, and I willed her to look at me. Her gaze met mine and held it for a moment. Adrenaline surged through my legs, a sensation in my thighs and knees that screamed to engage. My tongue trembled within my mouth. A single cicada began a song, and others joined in chorus, and her eyes moved past me.

She lay on her belly in the grass at the precipice and surveyed the bank. Sitting up, she unlaced her boots, wiping sweat from her face into her mud-colored hair. She tugged off her boots and socks and set them next to a tree trunk.

She slid again on her front, feet first, over the edge. Her toes were stubby and clumsy, kicking towards a clay and limestone ridge to find a foothold. I held my breath, willing her ungainly toes. When it did, I knew I wouldn't just watch her.

Her shirt caught under the weight of her torso and exposed the creamy softness of her stomach. She groaned and tried to free a hand to pull her shirt down, but couldn't without releasing her grip on the bank. Her cheeks flared into blushes. With a speed that indicated she no longer cared about her precariousness, she tumbled down, scraping her elbows and stomach on the mouth of the bank until she found the narrow lip of the pool and laid back against the wet, clay embankment walls to pull the shirt back into place. She was breathless. A ponytail of curly hair showed tiny curls knocked loose from her climb, making her round face cherubic.

She was awkward. The painful awkwardness of adolescence that makes adults look away, sometimes for years until a child blossoms, or grows out of it, or simply becomes ugly. Acne dappled her chin and forehead. Her fingers tugged across the hem of her shorts, willing them to cover her wide, muscular thighs. Her shirt stretched across her chest and belly, outgrown from last summer. But I thought she was beautiful. The beautiful potential of Annabel.

She didn't take off her clothes but slipped into the water like a sigh. It surprised me. It was the most graceful motion, as if she became dispossessed of her body and it belonged in the water with me. The coolness of the pool must have surprised her; she took a couple of quick inhales and let out a wicked, loud laugh.

Her arms and legs flailed, treading water at different rates until she found her equilibrium. She didn't look in my direction, near the trickle of the waterfall, under the edge, in the darkness. Instead she disappeared for a moment, her entire head going under the surface before she came back up with a gasp and her shirt in her hands. She threw it to the edge where she had entered the water. She wore a plain white bra that was translucent in the water. It was a taunt, a tease, a call.

With a blink, I disappeared beneath the surface. Her silhouette was headless below the water. She swam from one end of the pool to the other with slow, lazy kicks. The biological green of the water danced around her in glorious swirls, fish scattered, water striders darted from her on the surface. My lesser brethren resting under vegetation took notice of her.

I prodded a benign water snake from its domain under a large rock and watched it slide towards her. I heard a thin yell. Her kicks became vigorous, fat bubbles. As the snake swam downstream, I heard her laugh and her strokes slowed. I swam to the bottom of the pond. Above me, the sunlight streaked and was blotted out by her form across the surface.

She kicked and I grabbed her foot and held it in my hand. It was a delicate thing, so tiny and fragile. I pulled her under. Her legs took giant, hard kicks and I was impressed by their strength, how they entwined with mine. I could breathe her in through her skin against mine, as she
struggled and pushed. She screamed under the water. As the grasses swirled around her, I was paralyzed by the change in her complexion from pale to brown and green. Her dark eyes opened and met mine. Her body stilled and I let go.

By the time I surfaced she was already into the woods, her t-shirt slung across her neck. At the top of the bank, she sat down and put on her boots, watching me. I didn't hide. I don't know why. She didn't look away. I don't know why.

The sun was setting in the yellow summer sky when I saw her from underneath the water, climbing down the slope to the creek. Her steps were surer, her footholds remembered, her path clear. She made no move to get into the pool when she reached the water's edge. She lay on her stomach with her arms folded over the limestone. I emerged, my eyes barely above the surface. She found me and we stayed like that.

Slowly, she traced one of her fingers on the water and noticed the water skaters as they scattered. She smiled. I moved the water snake out of its home. She laughed and sat up.

"Do you control them?"

It was a question I wasn't expecting. "Not in the way that you think."

My voice was damp and muddy. She shivered at the sound of it. "Could you teach me?"

I blinked slowly and brought my voice down to a whispering rumble.

"Yes."

My afternoons that summer were filled with Annabel. Her body moving silently next to mine in the creek. Wet hair against her forehead, her eyes and nose above the water. Her breath rippling the surface, her dark eyes watching. I pretended that her gaze did not make my fingers throb with my own heartbeat as I stalked a small creature to devour, or prodded one animal into the jaws of another. The ebb and flow of the creek, the changes over the eons of my lifetime seemed to captivate her.

The more I saw of her, the more I wanted to be known by her. I yearned for her to look at me. I did not exist when she left and I roused with vibrant life when she came down the hillside. I hated needing her when she was gone.

I spent one morning waiting for her and she didn't come. The next day and the next. I tortured prey in the pool, stalking them but then becoming distracted by movement in the woods, only to miss them in the last moments of the hunt. I was hungry. I was so hungry for many things.

One morning I saw her body come down the hillside but I didn't dare leave the water. She called to me, teased me with words of apology. I could not see her past the hunger, past her fragile, tender body and translucent skin. Finally, she slipped into the water. I sprung. I kicked and flung myself across the pond in one bound, my fingers wrapping around her soft bobbing throat.

I could feel my pulse in the webbing of my fingers, itching in my legs. I could hear the cicadas' song rise into a frenzy and the creek water trickle around us and her breaths slowing, becoming longer and deeper.

Her smell was around me, touching me, melding with mine, connecting our songs. She put her lips to mine. She paused but I pushed through her hesitation and she returned my kiss. At first with a quick, darting tongue retreated back into her mouth but then with longer explorations, from the mild to the solicitous.

All at once she pressed into my body, her scratchy, wet bra and warm, firm breasts against me. An imbibing of each other, exploring flesh until we exhausted ourselves, panting and breaking apart clumsily. We rubbed our bodies together to the point of chafing. I pulled her closer and grazed the saltiness between her breasts with my tongue.  She blushed and pulled back.  With cheeks flaring she looked to the hillside of the surrounding woods. I followed her eyes and when I looked back to her, she un-hooked her bra and beckoned.

Holding onto the ledge, she tentatively kissed me again. When I pushed myself against her breasts, she did not pull back. I rolled down her shorts and she wrapped her legs around me. She moaned into my mouth and I caught her breath. She tortured me with a half-smile that brought me to a quick, shuddering convulsion. The deep, hot, sweet-ness remained and her legs twitched and she whimpered. I watched as her innocence seeped into the water and I sang, the deep vibrations filling us, echoing against the limestone walls. Her body flung over mine, the beauty of her awkwardness, the tender youth that I had captured, both pained and pleased me.

I believe we would have stayed like that, for hours, days, lifetimes but she heard a voice, her name. It called from beyond the trees and she stopped, pulling away quickly, panicked.

She lifted herself from the water, covering her chest with her shirt before putting her bra on underneath.

She scrambled to the top of the wall. She looked as if she wanted to say something, the words forming on her lips, but then she shook her head. I know I called to her, a gut-tural unrestrained sound and her lips quivered into a half-smile without looking at me. I kicked and landed on the creek bed with a squelching thud and she looked up at me. Her eyes widened and a convulsion shook her shoulders, shaking the droplets from her lips. She stared and watched me, then turned and raced up the hill.

◆

Oh, the emotions that ravaged me that night! Analyzing every action she took, how she didn't straighten her socks before pulling on her boots, how her shirt was inside out, the half-smile. That damn half-smile.

She didn't return the next day, or the next. I sang each evening for her, a deep and dreadful call that shook the trees and hushed the cicadas into a murmur. The nights were hot and I thrashed in my pool, wanting to leave, paralyzed with the need to stay, waiting. Waiting.

I fell into rumination during the night song. I replayed the memory of her toes as they looked for the limestone, stretched out until they grasped the surface. She was my complement, her smooth dryness caressing my slimy slickness, her naivety intoxicating my own guile. I could protect her in my world and her beauty would rule it. The sum-mer stars filled the sky as I sang.

She made her way down the hill so quietly that I didn't notice until loose rocks scattered into the pond. Her toe was reaching out, stretching to find the ledge. She sat on the ledge and crossed her legs, and I swam closer. Her eyes were red-rimmed and her cheeks puffy. Her throat was a bruise; greenish brown, like my own mottled skin.

"I want to hunt," Annabel said.

She undressed with a brutality, stripping down to an unabashed nakedness, and slipped into the pool. She dipped her head into the water next to me. Without my prompting, she chose a prey, a small frog croaking in the grass along the water's edge. Annabel fell mute, her patience taking up the cadence only known to those who stalk. My heart felt a sweetness, a bliss, watching her take possession of her savagery, welcoming my world as her own.

The stars shifted as we waited. The frog moved and Annabel grabbed, missed, stood up on a rock and scrambled over it. Her elbow smacked the stone but she dove as it wedged itself into a corner. She missed the frog with one hand but snatched it with the other. Her pupils dilated and she held it, pulsating.

Her body under the moonlight, her breasts dripping with water, her hair against her face, Annabel looked uncertain as she fought to hold on to the struggling creature. I moved behind her on top of the rock ledge. I don't know if I meant to save her from the decision every predator must make, or just bear witness. Her breaths came out in uneven gasps and she hesitated before shoving the frog into her mouth. She stiffened. Her eyes
flitted to the stars and then the water until her gaze settled on the reflection of herself with me behind her. Her throat bobbed and she retched. Her hands flew to the body of the frog, one pushing it into her mouth and the other clawing her throat. She swallowed.

The unfocused moon was sweating in the hot night air. Everything alive was fighting for space in the evening sky. The hum of the mosquitos countered the chirps of the crickets. The forest trembled with bats and owls, breaking the song only long enough for another performer to take up the next movement in the sonata.

I held her. She didn't move. I sang our song, and kissed her. She gagged and twisted away. Her arms flailed as she flung herself towards the rock, she shoved her knees into the clay ridge and scraped her legs as she clawed across the limestone. Annabel cried out in pain, but it mutated into a deep anguished cry. Her clothes were ignored while she kept her eyes on me, backing away. Pressing herself against the face of the rock, she raced up it, breasts grinding against shale, toes digging into clay, pushing towards the top.

It was Annabel who changed that night, not me. Her smell, the molecules she released into the air, what I sensed from her was no longer the awkward beauty, the innocent. And in that moment, I lashed out my tongue, the width of my head and the length of my body. It stuck to her with a squelch and retracted into me. It was then that memories poured into my mind, her smiles, her fevered moans. I recalled our words together, I repeated them, rearranged them. She struggled, half in my mouth, her muffled cries and bucking torso. I gagged but kept her inside me. Her strong, thick legs that swam in my creek, that wrapped around my torso as I emptied between us, now kicked into the air, looking for a ridge, a ledge, toes spread, outstretched, seeking something to catch her, and then they slowed, and stilled. I swallowed.

# Wakįyą

## Hanna Tawater

*"As a young man, he was shown the remains of a giant bird
that had been killed years before. As they explained the story,
for many months in the mid-19th century, before the Civil
War, an immense bird terrorized this pioneer community.
Many people encountered a bird that stood taller than a man.
Each wing was at least 8 feet long. Its color was gray, and it
gave off a suffocating odor. The bird was a threat to calves,
colts, dogs, deer, and children."*

- Mark A. Hall and Mark L Rollins, *Thunderbirds*

When I speak my lips clap thunder breaking inside a face in my face. Put on your humanskin, manbird, put on your snakeskin, shebird, snake into your twisted birdskin feather face my pretty pretty birdkin snakebird thundersonging inside a rib cage. I'm thundersonging you into a paper bone cage. Plucking featherscales for a regal headdress, Queen Ladybird of Fatter Clouds, Regent Stormpress of Snaketongues, sidewinding between lightning strikes, lightning beats in my electric bodysong.

Let me sing you a birdsong. ~

We were all birds once. (We were all snakes once.) But I was largest bird, (longest snake,) wicked black shadow twisted over mud, wicked black stain on paper. Feather or scale or woman or totem—we all dissolve, all mythsongs, scribed echolalia wet and thundering thundering. Until there is only quiet and drought, dried dirty mad.

But thundering, once, Snakebird or Devilbird, he called it, diving bird beneath water—sky hunted small frogmen, fishmen, swimming on grass conductors, burning grass houses, burning out the grass hypothalamus from your fishbrain, grass amygdala from your frogbrain. Devilbird snakebird controlled pain, will control your pain, a dampening lobotomy, sweet fishman with no fear swimming in a grass cloud, tugging at a fat drowned bird, water heavy, egg-clogged, cracking open electric currents trapped in this small bird body smoking featherscales.

But I was *large* once, snakenecked and leatherwinged, beaked and mailed. Once I dropped melvellei from a stormcloud clapping leviathan shaped wings leviathan shaped screams cracking open a sky. Giant whaleman plucked dropped plucked dropped plucked dropped plucked dropped, I made thunder with a body, made canyons with a monster, was the Whalequeen Stormbird, winged-she-snake-savior of the oceans.

But I was manshaped into wood, made a great totem posted in a dirt hole.

Wood wings make for poor thunder. Wood beaks make for a poorer hunger. ~


Nightraven flapping storms into terrorized juvenile silence, Nightheron prey on a water's edge fishman fishing, goat-sucking Nighthawk diving to a winged boom—Lady Nightjar thundergrounded. (We flew, we flew so fast, so hard, to be so groundborne.) Tawny frogmouth, rapid beakless breathing chasing frogmen to a fragile nest for roosting, for basking, a thermoregulated snakebird in the most delicate pit of twigs trying trying and bringing no storm.

I am not your many colored crow—making no sacrifices scorching no plumage for you I bring rain, rain, rain and not fire. I *am* Devilbird bloodscreaming from a black black air. I *am* Curtiss Shrike combatscreeching butcherbird posting frogs on spikes. I *am* thunderbird or harpy, always villainous, always wild terror, he said, in need of ribcaging hollow bones poking inwards—domesticated—pulled from the sky, dressed in black and white, stationed at a desk bored gussied up secretarybird with painted eyes. A safer space for saving.

And the grass began to dry. ~


They put us in paper cages, our papery bones too brittle for breaking. But we were romance—bird as motif. Then birds as lovers, and last bird as mangod, prince as bird, skulking through a forest, manbird in manskin needing, needing, to save as we save in our snakeskin ladyshape. Snakes were birds once, I was a bird once raining on everything, I was a potnia theron once—the difference between goddess and common—the difference between goddess and harpy is what order the spare parts are attached. Princess birdbrain with tits. But no one wants to fuck a womanfaced birdbody, so I was white-shaped into a monster story, villainous, villainous, and monsters are made for saving.

But we weren't meant for grounding, legs pinned rearwards, ungainly and hopeless on land red-throated waterbird with wax skin, we could only float. Slower fowl for chasing brighter targets for hunting fatter fauna for feasting and you can't feast on storms.

You wanted me a pretty white and yellow meadowlark, small plains-bound and not red-throated red-headed red-shouldered red-winged red-breasted red-bellied red-tailed sitting singing sweetly on a kitchen window sill. You wanted me a prairie rose North Dakotan housewife, fishwife, fable not red reptilian winged she-beast because you know you can't hide from things that fly. You can't hide from storms.

So we were snakeshaped into silent she-beasts, repetitious curves in a hard dusty ground. ~


Pretty as a bird and that bird's a snake, we were snakes once, given the sky. So we brought clouds, brought thunder— *wakíya* means sacredbird, thunderbird, sacred-she-storm, we were precious once. We were untamed, pulling beaks back to open our she-face, face in my face, pulling back our birdskin to bear our she-skin. But they took every feather, leaving only scales, close enough he said—Manbird noble Princebird scooping small beak snake, sweet small ladysnake twisting through rough plumage, down getting caught on our serrated edges. Close enough he said, parched, but snakes are venomous. We made things grow, once, you know.

We don't get to be birds anymore. ~


It doesn't rain anymore.

# RIVER RUN

## Tina Hyland

*"'The legend is picturesque enough,' observed the Doctor after one of the longer pauses, speaking to break it rather than because he had anything to say, 'for the Wendigo is simply the Call of the Wild personified, which some natures hear to their own destruction.'"*

- Algernon Blackwood, *The Wendigo*

"I guess we did go the wrong way," Kyle said.

That "we" always got to her. As though it were their mutual responsibility when things went wrong. He had insisted that this was the right way. Had he been correct, he would have basked in it, no "we" for miles. But blame, that was his favorite thing to share.

"I told you that hours ago," she said.

He turned on his phone and held it in the air again, searching for a signal. Carly didn't know how far they had walked, all at his insistence that he recognized some particular copse of trees. She had told him, more than once, that using a tree as a landmark in the woods was about as effective as using a streetlight in Minneapolis. He told her that she needed a better attitude, that she was making it more difficult. The attitude argument was one of his favorites, as if cheerfully following his instincts and ignoring her own would have made it better. If she smiled more, they wouldn't be lost at all.

The sunlight came in at a long angle, thinned by the growing shadows of trees. The bushes rustled with small animals. Each sound made her jump and peer into the woods. Crows gathered to roost, sweeping the sky in black, shrieking like omens.

"This is some Blair Witch shit," she said.

Kyle stopped and took her hands in his. He looked in her eyes with that cinematic sap face she had grown to loathe. Romance was coming, thick syrupy globs of it.

"Carly, everything is going to be ok, I swear. I would never let anything to happen to you." Each word was perfectly enunciated, the face, overdrawn with emotion. As if he were waiting for the camera to pan upward, above the screaming crows, to show them standing in the pin-drop center of an immense wood, no roads in frame. This was a setting for heroics, for winning back the girl, where the problems they'd been having all vanished in these moments of real danger. Their squabbles made petty as he saved her life, despite all the ways she didn't deserve it or him. It was his proving ground. His woodland rescue action flick. He was always acting.

"Hey," Kyle said. "That looks like it would fit in your garden."

He pointed to a mossy log, its underside probably rotten and hollowed by insects. And if it wasn't full of rot and maggots, did he think they could drag it through the woods?

"We should find some food and make a fire before it gets dark," she said.

He turned away, disappointed. She was cranky, but he was incompetent and sappy, and that, she thought, was a good summary of their relationship.

"Ok," he said. "I'll find food, you find wood."

They had eaten the last granola bar, split in half, that morning, and her stomach grumbled. Carly kicked around the brush, pissed off and hungry. Hiking wasn't her thing, never had been, but Kyle insisted on it. It should have been a day trip, but he had led her away from the trail to see some rumored petroglyphs. Some real wilderness. Romance. Adventure. They never found the petroglyphs. She saw a doe and a fawn, but all she could think about was ecosystems, food chains. If there were bambis in the woods, there were things to eat them. Mosquitos whirred around her, a cloud of them. She slapped one on her shoulder.

"Ah," she said. "Nature."

She snapped twigs to see if they were dry. The brittle cracking sound pleased her. The use of force, the act of breaking something, pleased her. The most satisfying moment of two days was brutalizing sticks.

She waved the mobbing mosquitos away, tried to be calm, thought about the idea of calmness in this situation and laughed, loud and cruel.

"You say something?" Kyle called out.

"Nope. Just thinking about dying out here."

"You're not gonna die out here."

"Ok," Carly said. Her voice was sweet and mocking. The bitchiness of it made her smile and she regretted it. She took a deep breath, hissed at a mosquito on her arm before she flattened it with her palm and flicked its body on the ground.

Kyle was building a stone ring for the fire when she got back. He smiled and took the pile of wood from her arms. "I found you something," he said.

He walked to a tree and picked up a pile of wild strawberries. Carly wondered how many he had eaten. She didn't want to wonder things like that, to be the kind of person who is pissy and suspicious.

"Thanks," she said. Carly took the handful of berries and tried not to devour them, to savor them slowly. Kyle built a pyramid of wood and piled some dry pine needles in the center. Carly smirked at how textbook it was, how boyscout. Last night he had used all of her lighter fluid, and she wondered how this would go.

It took him a few tries, but he got the fire started, and Carly tried to feel grateful. She tried to feel anything about him that wasn't shitty and cruel, but even the curls of hair that fell in his face and the way he tucked them back with his hand, the way he took a big, heaving breath before he spoke, the way he kept turning his phone on and off, the way he pulled up his jeans every few minutes, the way he pursed his lips when, of course, there was still no signal, the way he kept saying "in theory" this or "in theory" that about how they could find a road or a town by one half-remembered woodland survival fact or another, all of it, his every gesture and sound, pissed her off. Carly lit her last cigarette.

Kyle walked over and sat down. He put his arm around her shoulder and it felt like a worm, like something vile but she didn't cringe. Carly stiffened.

"We really are going to be ok," he said.

"You keep saying that."

"Because it's true."

She could feel he was trying to give her the sap eye and she scowled at the ground, refusing to let it happen.

"Same routine as last night?" she asked. The one thing she had been able to demand, to win, was that they sleep in shifts. She wanted the light of the fire and to know he was listening for bears or wolves or whatever else the woods contained while she tried to sleep.

Kyle took his arm down. "You want to sleep first or should I?"

"I'm pretty tired."

"Then you first."

r

*Carly was standing in the woods, calling to him, to Kyle. She heard him call back, some-where further, deeper, where there was no moonlight. Carly called to him and he called back. She followed the sound. Whispers rose at her flank and she snapped her head around to find them, held out her arms in the darkness. Ghost-white figures smiled at her and turned away. When they turned, they disappeared. Carly called to him and he called back, deeper and further. He was singing, she followed the singing. "Everybody's got a hungry heart. Lay down your money and you play your part. Everybody's got a hu-hu-hungry heart." The whispers were louder, ghost-white men turning in front of her, appearing and disappearing, smiling with teeth long and sharp.*

r

It was fully dark when Carly woke up to pee. The fire was in embers.
She stood up and Kyle was across the fire ring, rolling and groaning on the ground.

She shouted his name. He moaned.

Kyle sat up straight and sudden, unnatural, his waist swinging upward at a hinge. His head turned slowly to her, turned too far, turned on a dowel.

"Are you sick?" she asked carefully.

Kyle stood up and walked over to her. He took her arm and she felt her skin prickle. She shuddered.

He pulled her forearm up to his mouth and kissed it. He kissed it again, and she could feel the wetness of his tongue.

She pulled her arm back but he gripped it tight. He bit her, hard. She heard the skin break open.

Carly screamed and wrenched her arm away. She could see her blood darker on their silhouettes. She was scared to feel the bite, the divot of skin, but she felt the blood dripping steadily down her fingertips, saw the rivulets of blacker black on her arm and his chin. She looked between the arm and Kyle, tried to make sense of it. The arm pulsed, blood pulsed. Kyle crouched down low and she backed away. He picked up a pile of leaves and held it to his nose, took a deep smell of it. He licked the leaves, her blood off the leaves. He smiled, face splitting, parting too wide.

He reached for her again and she kicked him, a crack across the head. He fell to the ground and reached for her ankles. She jumped easily out of the way.

She needed a weapon. She grabbed one of the rocks at the edge of the fire and it scalded her hand. She screamed and let go and she heard Kyle make a sound. It was the rustling of leaves, or twigs snapping underfoot. It was the hiss of something wild and dangerous.

She ran.

The moon gave a dim glow to the woods, but tree limbs still scratched at her face and arms. She picked her feet up high. If she fell, if she tripped, Kyle wasn't Kyle anymore. He was something else. He would kill her. Sweet, sappy, incompetent Kyle.

The thing that had been Kyle howled. She ran faster. Her foot caught a log and she tumbled hard to the ground. She was back up in an instant.

Limbs tore at her hair, scratched her in the eye. Tears blurred the darkness. Carly kept going. She heard the sound of water and remembered yesterday, when Kyle said, "In theory, if we found a river, we could probably follow it to town. All the towns up here were built on rivers." Kyle didn't know how to swim. She had tried for a whole summer, to coax him into lakes. He was even scared of her family's slow rolling pontoon boat, always wore a life jacket, always looked uneasy in her mom's pictures.

She jumped in the water and splashed to the middle where it was deepest. She was relieved to feel the ground disappear from under her. She could swim fast, underwater, quietly. Just come up when she had to. Kyle wouldn't follow her in the water, and the river would carry her faster than he could run.

The current was strong, swollen from rain. It spat her out toward the edge of the river but she wanted to stay far from the banks. Far from him. She swam against it, felt the sting of the muddy water on the bite. The current pinned her hard against a fallen tree. She tried to swim under it, but the limbs caught her shirt. She had followed sweet, dopey Kyle into the woods, and now he wanted to kill her, to eat her, and she had escaped, found the safety of water. Now she would drown in it. Her shirt was caught up, her head underwater. She flailed and tore at the shirt, pulled it over her head and left it. She choked and gasped for breath, splashing in the current. Her body tumbled through the flows and she tried to breathe, caught swallows of gritty water.

The river flattened to shallow rapids, full of stones, her head cracked against them. Carly stood up and ran, slipping over mossy stones, trying to find deeper water. She tripped again, came down hard, her head striking a boulder, her vision fuzzy.

Kyle stood over her and she tried to push herself away, back to the safety of deep water. Better to drown, she thought. He walked easily over the stones. She floundered and fell again, this time her ankle twisting, snapping and she howled. Kyle howled back. In the moonlight, he was pale, skin a hollow white, eyes glowing.

Kyle crouched over her.

He held a stone over his head, smooth and dark, rounded by the rapids. It glinted, she could see it had a vein of quartz. A rock she would have picked up and kept in her garden.

The rock smashed down between her eyes.

# THE SOUTH

ARKANSAS ◼ THE FOUKE MONSTER
## OLD FOUKEY

VIRGINIA ⬥ THE BUNNY MAN
## FLESH AIR

TENNESSEE ▬ THE BELL WITCH
## A LITTLE TEMPLE

# OLD FOUKEY

## Alex Bosworth

*"Fouke Monster-mania has died down in recent years, but in 1998 there was a rash of over fourty sightings, with twenty-two of them in a single day! Had monster-mania reached a fever pitch again and affected the collective imagination of this small rural community? Or is it possible that there really is a strange subhuman beast lurking in the backwoods of Arkansas?"*

- Mark Moran and Mark Sceurman, *Weird U.S.*

"A lot of strange things go on in those bottoms." says Sheriff Dwayne Hawkins, placing his index finger on a brownish-green area of his map of Fouke County. "Those bottoms hold a lot of secrets." Hawkins is referring to a sedimentary flood plain created by the Sulfur River in Southwest Arkansas known to locals as "the bottoms". This soggy stretch of wilderness and swampland surrounds Fouke County where Hawkins has served as a law officer for nearly forty years.

According to rumors that began before Fouke County was even established, the outlying marshes in that section of the state are home to the legendary "Fouke Monster", also known as the "Southern Sasquatch", "Old Foukey", "The Foukmeister General" and occasionally "Mr. Peebles" for reasons as mysterious as the creature itself.

Sheriff Hawkins is probably the best authority when it comes to this territory and possibly the only reliable eyewitness to the existence of an enigmatic creature lurking in its bogs and wetlands. "I wouldn't say it lurks, exactly," says Hawkins. "I'm not even sure what constitutes lurking outside of a literary reference. I've seen the monster walking around. I've seen him hang out for a while. One time, I might even have hauled him in for loitering if he weren't so imposing." Hawkins goes on to describe the Fouke creature as roughly eight and a half feet tall with an enormous, apelike body. The beast is reportedly covered entirely with hair except for a thinning area on its scalp. "That's why we say 'he' when we talk about the monster. Male pattern baldness," Dwayne reports. "That and his enormous penis. You could wave out a campfire by swinging that thing once or twice."

Hawkins drives me to a farm just east of town. "I took one of the first calls about Old Foukey back in '75, when I was a new deputy," he tells me along the way. "I went out here to Wayne Forrester's place to investigate an incident involving some slaughtered livestock. Horrible thing to see. The night before, something had smashed through a gate and two fences, got ahold of a couple of goats, pushed their heads together so hard it pretty much flattened them. Then it rips one of their legs off and beats a pig to death with it. The thing rips open the pig and uses its entrails to choke a lamb. We think the mother came over to protect her young one, 'cause the creature just punched that sheep right into the ground. Then it stuck its arm down her throat and pulled out her liver."

We're greeted at the Forrester farm by Wayne and his wife, Elaine. The elderly couple politely walks us out to a spot a hundred yards from their house. "We heard some kind of strange howling noise, so I come out here with the flashlight," Wayne states, pointing to a nearby field. "And here's this thing, looks like a King Kong, just sitting there, chomping down on something. I put the light on it, but it didn't seem to care, just kept on eating."

The sheriff says that apparently, after killing the mature sheep, the monster simply sat down on the lamb's body feasting on its mother's fresh liver.

"I fired off a shot with the rifle to scare it away." Elaine says.

"Didn't budge." Wayne adds. "After a while, it just got up, whizzed on what was left of the pig and wandered off into the dark holding a goat carcass in one of its hands."

"Its hands are massive." Sheriff Hawkins says as we head back into town. "But the prints we've taken show that its feet are deceptively small. That's why I never call this thing Bigfoot. This creature has tiny, delicate feet. I believe it has the feet of a dancer."

The first time Hawkins encountered Old Foukey himself was in the summer of 1977. "I was responding to a call about some missing campers in the Boggy Creek area," Hawkins tells me as he pours us both some coffee. "As I headed down a trail to some campsites about three miles off the main road, I saw this enormous guy squatting behind a fallen oak tree. He was facing away and I could only see his top half, but I could tell he must have been over seven feet tall. I pulled over to take a look. When he'd finished his business, he stood up and saw me in my car and started grunting and howling real loud. That's when I realized this was the monster who'd torn all those animals asunder at the Forrester place. I ran the siren and flashed the lights. He picked up the fallen tree he'd been using as a crapper and tossed it in my direction, taking out the front of my patrol car. I exited the vehicle, pulled out my sidearm and began firing. He started looking around for another tree. As he began uprooting another oak to throw at me, I proceeded on foot away from the scene. He chased me most the way back to the highway," Hawkins says with a laugh as he takes a sip from his cup. "Never did find those campers."

In the following years, Deputy Dwayne became Sheriff and during his tenure in that position he's sighted the Fouke Monster on half a dozen occasions by his count. "This one time in '81, I saw him behind the Second Offense bar and grill just before midnight and I swear he was rocking out to a song that was playing on the jukebox inside. It was something by The Eagles. Man, did he like that sound! About ten years later, I saw Old Foukey at a picnic site near the river and I popped in a Don Henley CD I had in the car to see if he'd like it. But when he heard it, Old Foukey just walked away shaking his head as if he found the music self-indulgent and pretentious."

Local feed store owner, Lane Jefferson claims that the Fouke creature has had several encounters with his former wife, Jane Jefferson Higgins. "That thing cornered her in the barn on at least three occasions that I know of!" Lane states angrily. "God only knows what he did to her in there! She won't even talk about it! But the whole thing ruined our relationship. She never looked at me the same way after that."

The former Mrs. Jefferson, who still lives at their farm, could not be reached for comment, although she has been quoted by many in the area as saying that Old Foukey was "certainly a beast, but no monster", "surprisingly gentle for his girth" and "a mysterious rogue whose thinning mane belies the virility of a warrior with a powerfully throbbing heart." Since the divorce, Lane has formed several hunting parties in hopes of wreaking vengeance on the Fouke creature. "We've got to kill that hairy, unnaturally-proportioned bastard!"

But perhaps the most well-known story about the Fouke Monster involves retired bartender, Shane Fuller. Fuller was fishing on Lake Pierce at the east end of the county on May 24, 1988. He had just pulled his boat onto shore when the Fouke Monster emerged from the woods, no doubt intrigued by the string of catfish the old man was carrying. Legend has it that the creature hit Fuller with such a forceful blow that it tore his head clean off. Of course with legends, there is often great exaggeration. The evidence shown in the autopsy suggests that Fuller's head was slowly pulled off over a period of ten to fifteen minutes. "The human head is pretty well connected to the body," said Fouke County Coroner, Payne Hauser. "It takes a load of yanking to get that thing off." Both the coroner and Sheriff Hawkins concluded that Old Foukey held Fuller between its powerful thighs and either twisted his head off or simply yanked it free from Fuller's torso. The head itself was later found at a nearby playground in the net of a basketball hoop.

"We may never know what's wandering around out there," Hawkins says with a shrug and a sigh of resignation. "But from what I've seen, it just wants to be left alone to poke around the bottoms, grab itself something to eat and pay a visit to the Jefferson's barn once in a while."

The Sheriff leans back in his chair, placing his boots on the desk. "Besides, he's hardly the worst one in his family."

# FLESH AIR

## Jim Ruland

*"The legend gets a little unclear once again with respect to the fate of the Bunnyman. Some say that when police finally tracked him down, he ran onto the tracks of an oncoming train, killing himself. Others say he just vanished into the woods, never to be seen (alive) again. The Bunnyman's body has never been found."*

- Dave Waldin, *Weird Virginia*

The smell is always with me. The wind blows from the river and the stench seeps out of me: old filth and new blood, sweetness sitting on top of decay. When it's bad, there's nothing I can do but sit and listen to my tapes until the bad feeling passes. If it passes... Wait... Hold on....

It all started when my daddy was sent away and momma packed me off to Galaxy to spend the summer with my granddaddy in the big old house he calls his hundred-year house on account of how old it is. It stands at the top of a long rise that trickles down to the river, the oldest in Virginia, or so I'm told.

Galaxy has a weird smell. That's how it seems to me, the prodigal son, back from the suburbs, accustomed to paved roads and lawns that get mowed in the summer and raked in the fall. Galaxy is a different kind of town, and it smells different, too. I don't know if it's from the chemical spill in the river all those years ago, but it stinks. There is something rotten about the place.

Galaxy gets a lot of rain, summer showers are a daily occurrence, and an abundance of greenery flourishes. The grass and shrubs and trees all grow tall and strong and in most places are shrouded with kudzu. They call it Virginia creeper here, a tough green vine that can climb just about anything and chokes the life out of all that it seeks to claim, a reminder that all living things must someday die, either of its own accord or with a little help from Mother Nature.

That's all for now. My batteries are running low.

My room is on the top floor in what was once an attic. The ceiling slopes on both sides right down the middle of the room. The mattress is soft and musty and the springs make a lot of noise when I get in and out of bed. Sometimes I can even hear the sound on my tapes.

My granddaddy is always complaining about the noise, especially that first summer. He wasn't used to having anybody in the house with him. I would lay in bed at night in the sticky heat as if paralyzed, staring at the patterns on the wallpaper, afraid to make a sound.

My bedroom faces the backyard and from my window I can see most of my granddaddy's property. The window sits directly above the covered patio where my granddaddy likes to smoke and read the papers. I can hear him down there early in the morning and deep into the evening, coughing and spitting into a can. A green lawn slopes down to a wild-looking garden where he grows tomatoes and cucumbers and kale, which I don't care for. I don't like to go down there because on the other side of the garden is the foul-smelling ditch of a creek that smells like a sewer no matter how high or low it runs, especially in the heat of the day. On the other side of the ditch is a long narrow field filled with tall grass hedged in on either side by a line of towering rhododendrons that runs all the way down to the river, and in the center of this meadow sits an unusually large rabbit hutch. That's where I met the Bunny Man.

I only saw him once that first summer, but I heard about him a lot. My granddaddy was a mostly agreeable fellow who kept to himself and liked it that way. He didn't go to church or take dinners with his neighbors. Once, in the grocery store, where everyone talked to everyone, he had a word with just about every man he met, but at the house he wasn't nearly as gregarious. He gave me a list of chores he expected me to do and rules to follow, which included Bible study in the evening. *You be a good boy*, my granddaddy cackled, *or I'll send you to the Bunny Man.*

It was hot and stuffy in the attic and I spent a lot of time sitting by the window, listening to people talk on the radio. There was one show that was nothing but reports about the effects of the chemical spill on the river. People from the surrounding towns called in with stories of fish kills, two-headed water moccasins and frogs with so many legs they looked like big green spiders. Sometimes I'd shut off the radio and record the cicadas droning in the trees like some kind of alien machine. When I play these tapes back, sometimes I hear things I missed during the recording, and the sound takes on the shape of a song. My daddy likes these tapes, says they remind him of home.

One evening, shortly before dusk toward the end of the summer, I watched a man dressed in dark coveralls come up from the river to the rabbit hutch. He was a long way off and his hair hung down in his face so I couldn't see him very clearly, but he carried something that hung limp in his hand like a sack or a shirt or perhaps a fish or some other dead thing. He pulled open the door to the hutch and disappeared inside. I waited as darkness fell for him to come out, but he never did.

My momma bought me a new tape recorder for my birthday and I brought both of them with me to Galaxy that second summer to keep me entertained during the long lonely evenings after my chores were done. I started to record and edit my own programs. Sometimes I'd pretend to be a talk show host or a news anchor or a broadcaster for make-believe sports teams and horse racing derbies. I made up the names of players and their stats, jockeys and their thoroughbreds. I'd invent calamities and uprisings at the place where my daddy was locked up. And then I'd say, "Back to you, Steve." And then I'd say "Thank you, Dale. You keep cool out there."

Around about July I decided I wanted to interview a real person. My granddaddy had fallen into one of his quiet periods where he mostly sat on the patio, tapping a rolled up newspaper on his leg. He did this so often and so insistently that both his hands and his trousers were black with ink, and pages of the newspaper were torn and frayed so that it resembled a shaggy club. I thought I'd go to the Galaxy Market and ask people about the weather, or the river—something everyone seemed to have an opinion about—but then the Bunny Man returned.

I hadn't seen him in almost a year, and from my perch in the window he seemed unchanged: same dark coveralls, same long hair, same unkempt appearance; but I saw him much more frequently now. He came to the hutch nearly every day. Hauling feed, emptying waste, tinkering with his tools. He installed a table outside the hutch and every third or fourth day he'd skin a rabbit. He'd separate the creature from its hide as quickly as I could peel an orange. He'd cure the skins and put the meat in a small covered pot that he'd take away with him to the river, always to the river. That's when it came to me: I'll interview the Bunny Man.

The next morning I erased a tape with some of my more amateur efforts, replaced the batteries in my new recorder, and headed down to the yard. I was surprised to see my granddaddy working in the garden, whistling a tune I couldn't quite catch. He had a clutch of big red tomatoes in a basket, and he seemed to be in a good mood. When my daddy got through with one of his dark spells, he could be like this, too: happy and cheerful; but the slightest thing could set him off. I learned to be careful in both deed and word. I didn't think it was a good idea to tell my granddaddy my plans, but he took one look at the tape recorder slung over my shoulder by its leather strap and guessed my intent. *You think you gone catch a Bunny Man with that?*

It wasn't a question I knew the answer to.

He handed me the basket while he went back to work. I picked up one of the tomatoes, turned it over in my hand. Its backside was covered in black spores. Something shifted inside and I dropped it on the ground. The tomato didn't split but one of the spots ruptured and a fat white worm pushed through the hole. It wasn't a maggot or a grub, but a long eyeless snake the length of my forearm. My granddaddy brought his boot down on the worm and stomped it flat with a savagery I knew all too well. It was in the blood he passed down to my daddy and my daddy done passed down to me.

When my granddaddy was finished he took the basket and examined every tomato. Some of the spots were dark and some were faint, but they all had them. Every single one. I thought of the tomatoes I'd eaten with my lunch the day before, the slick red slices glistening with oil and salt, and with the stench rising from the ditch I felt like something was uncoiling in more places than my imagination. My granddaddy took off his hat and pulled off his gloves and dropped them in the soil as he made his way down the row and back to the hundred-year house.

To get to the field I had to cross the ditch. Though I've seen it marked on maps as Galaxy Creek it seldom runs stronger than a trickle, even during the rains, but is never dry. The ditch bottom is as mucky as any swamp and swarming with all manner of bugs and fish and critters that had retreated from the diseased river. A large pipe served as a bridge and I made my way across, my balance thrown off by the weight of the tape recorder.

I cleared the creek and when I looked up, there he was, The Bunny Man, looking down at me, his eyes like pieces of flint in the bottom of a tangled nest. *What you want?* he asked, his voice flat but accusatory. He used one hand to brush his hair from his eyes, the other held a sharpened piece of steel he used to beat the weeds down.

*I want to talk to you,* I said, holding out the recorder like it held the answer to his question. *You want to talk to me with that thing?* I nodded that I did. He asked me if it was for school and I told him that it was, even though it was summer, and if he'd asked me where I went to school I wouldn't have been able to name one within a hundred miles. He smiled, a bright white smile that showed he was younger then I'd thought, closer to my daddy's age than my granddaddy's. *Okay*, he said, *but we gonna do it in there.* He pointed at the hutch with the piece of steel that looked like a broken lawnmower blade. I was scared to go in there, but just as scared not to.

Outside the hutch on the Bunny Man's bench lay a dead rabbit. Skinned except for his feet. I tried not to look at it as I followed the Bunny Man to the hutch, which had several doors but only one large enough for a person to squeeze through. Even so he had to hunch down as he lifted himself up and turn his body sideway to get through the door, and I followed. Inside it was dark and loud and packed with rabbits. Cages were stacked from floor to ceiling six high and each one was stuffed with the creatures. There must have been hundreds of rabbits in there. Many of them cried out at me like a chorus of frightened babies, a terror so great there was no way to stifle it.

Then there was the smell. Urgent and overwhelming. The sharp ammoniac smell of urine lay on top of the stink of too many rabbits in too small a place. The stench filled my mouth and nose, like I was breathing in air furred with flesh and fear. *I gotta get out of here,* I thought, over and over again, but the shameful truth was I was too scared to move.

The Bunny Man sat me down on the floor that was littered with drifts of fur and hard pellets I hoped was feed. The Bunny Man sat down across from me on a pile of skins. There were skins everywhere. They were stapled to the ceiling and covered the walls. There were so many I could not find a place on the wall that was not skin nor could I tell what was animal and what was skin and it seemed as if the walls were full of teeth and eyes.

He sat down beside a shelf crowded with vials of liquid, pans of powder, and bits and bones tied up with colorful ribbon and string. Many hundreds of feet that looked like claws dangled from the ceiling. I fumbled with the recorder, speaking into the microphone, playing it back. *Check, check, one, two, three.*

*That thing on?* he asked and when I told him it was, he began. *Your granddaddy hired me to keep the rabbits out of the garden. So I built this place so they'd have a place to live. I don't believe a thing should be killed for its own sake, you understand?* I said that I did but my throat felt clogged. *I'm sorry*, he said though it was clear he was anything but. *Would you like something to drink?* he asked, his tone formal and mocking. I shook my head. *I can brew you some Bunny Man tea!* The hutch shook with his laughter, which spread through the cages like a current so that the squealing of the rabbits and the rattling of the cages rose in intensity. I took it all in, the potions and the bones. His legion of rabbits. *He's a witch*, I thought. *The Bunny Man is a witch.* The realization came upon me all of a sudden. I watched the wheels on the tape machine turn in slow circles. One time, two times, and on three I bolted, leaving the recorder behind.

That night a cold front moved in over the mountains and my granddaddy built a fire in the kitchen and I stayed with him for a while. He told me he knew the Bunny Man was strange, and he'd done a good job, but there was no keeping the wrongness of what was in the river from polluting the place. I didn't say nothing about his tomatoes and he didn't ask me about my recorder, why I didn't have it with me, where it had gone to. He called me Karl, and I wondered if he thought he was talking to my daddy.

The rains came. I didn't see the Bunny Man for the rest of the summer.

When I came back to Galaxy this summer, the recorder lay on my bed. It was dented and dirty, its buttons worn from use, but the batteries are fresh and the tape new. When I pressed play, it was nothing but rabbits. 90 minutes, 45 to a side, of rabbits squealing and shrieking in that infernal way they do. I listened to the whole thing, waiting for a message to appear, but there wasn't any. In a way, that's a kind of message. Like the way my daddy and I talk to each other and make our intentions known on the tapes we send each other, even when its just recordings of cicadas or doors slamming or men crying.

My granddaddy is in a bad way. He doesn't call me Karl no more. He barely talks at all. His eyes focus but don't see. The edge of the afterlife bleeds into his visions. Memories from the past, memories of you, daddy.

Every morning I find a new tape. On the porch. In the mailbox. Tucked inside an envelope tied to the tomato cages that hold up the withered stalks of my granddaddy's ruined garden. Every one of them is the same. Rabbits, rabbits, rabbits. Every single one.

⚓

The rains have come early this year. The clouds are fast moving, the rain fierce. The thunder comes down right on top of me and I can feel the lightning wanting to come down. I have always liked the feel of that super-charged air flowing through me. I would welcome a strike, to be touched by one of God's stray thoughts. I would accept that power. I will need it when the skies clear and the timber dries and it is time for me to strike the rabbit hutch down, to burn up the fields, all the way down to the river, and the river, too, if need be. There is too much that is rotten here, too much disease. I hear your voice inside me. I know what you're calling on me to do. Just tell me when, daddy, and I will light the fire and cleanse these fields, purify the river, burn this hundred-year-house and all of Galaxy to the ground.

# A LITTLE TEMPLE

## Kiik A.K.

*"In 1819, reports of the "Bell Witch" reached Nashville, Tennessee. Andrew Jackson, future president and hero of the War of 1812, heard the ghost stories. Interested, he traveled to the Bell farm, intending to drive away the evil spirit, or prove it to be a hoax. But the Bell Witch terrorized Jackson, and he left within two days. He was quoted as saying, 'I'd rather fight the British in New Orleans than have to fight the Bell Witch.'"*

- Sue L. Hamilton, *Ghosts and Goblins*

<u>ALTERNATE TITLES</u>
The Bell Jar
Bell & The Beast
Bell Witchy Woman
The Bell Witch & The Grundle
Of Witches & Grundles
Bell and Her Grundlekin
When Bell Met the Gundmeister
Witches, Grundles & a Mortgage
The Bell Witch of the Ball
Belly & Grundy
Kate!
Tennessee City, Tennessee
Buzzard Creek, TN
Red River City
Burning Love . . . & Witches
Life at the Stake
witch
WITCH!!

*Present day. We're in a cramped, shabby home. A mansion of stains. The three most common locations will be the bedroom, the kitchen and the living room. If there are pillows nearby the stuffing must be protruding from their corners.*

KATE BATTS is a pretty, middle-aged woman. Conservative, worn, faded attire. You get the feeling she cuts her own hair. She is also THE BELL WITCH. Please call Jane Adams. If Jane Adams is unavailable please call Carrie-Anne Moss. Carrie-Anne is a little too tall though so please if you can ask her to perform her scenes "a little smaller."

THE GRUNDLE is a common grundle. Please call Patton Oswalt. But he can't be clean Patton. Dirty, sweat-absorbed Patton. Stomachflu-for-two-straight-weeks Patton. It isn't enough simply to watch him with our eyes. We need to SMELL him with our eyes. Patton Oswalt must be squeezed into an opossum suit that is both terrifyingly-intricate and two sizes too small. Sometimes he wears a loosened tie, as though winding down from a day at work.

## I.

Kate and The Grundle are getting into shape. Living room furniture has been pushed aside to accommodate pilates mats. Workout clothes cling uncomfortably. The two are darkened with sweat.

On their tv a workout video entitled *Abs of Titans*. The DVD jacket is nearby looking like a little temple. It is adorned with images of tropical flowers, a burning sunrise and a nude man, flexing, carved from stone.

Kate gasps as though having a heart attack and imitates the workout instructions weakly. The Grundle has stopped exercising altogether. He has his head propped up on a foam roller and stares ahead at the tv.

### KATE SAYS
Are you planning on more pilates or are you only going to ogle the video hostess in her spandex for the next hour.

### THE GRUNDLE SAYS
I asked you not to pick a DVD with an attractive fitness host. I can't barely concentrate on my technique and then I injure myself. I don't say things like that to make you jealous.

### KATE SAYS
So this is my fault. Because there was a vast selection of fitness experts who looked like Chris Farley I intentionally avoided.

### THE GRUNDLE SAYS
I've pulled my back out. My extremities are throbbing. And I have a dehydration migraine.

### KATE SAYS

Oh god. And I suppose his royal vagina is sore too. From all the talking he does out of it.

### THE GRUNDLE SAYS

Why do you insult me in the third-person? I'm here in front of you. I'm dying. I feel like my body is submerged in hot lava.

### KATE SAYS

That is what exercise is supposed to feel like. When you yank your muscles into excruciating pain it means you're getting them like way better.

### THE GRUNDLE SAYS

I don't need my muscles to get way better. I just need the surface of my body to stop burning at hemorrhoid-level sensitivity.

### KATE SAYS

Maybe you should stop focusing on how painful exercise is and instead on how hardened your arteries get after you eat two cylinders of girl scout cookies for breakfast.

### THE GRUNDLE SAYS

Are you being my motivational speaker now? Is that what is happening here?

### KATE SAYS

Who said anything about your motivation? I'm clearly just shaming you.

### THE GRUNDLE SAYS

You're lucky my legs are too numb for me to get up and pack a suitcase. I'd make you a middle-aged divorcee in about six seconds.

### KATE SAYS

Like you have anywhere to go. Make sure you pack about thirty boxes of cheese crackers in your luggage. You'll need enough nutrition to get you past the next ten hours before you get lightheaded.

### THE GRUNDLE SAYS

Why do I let you choose what we do on Sunday mornings? I'm going to start going to church.

### KATE SAYS

Shut it up and finish your damn crunches.

## II.

Kate and The Grundle are babysitting. Kate's nieces are very stupid, very fat twin babies. Kate is rocking STUPID BABY ONE to sleep. She sings a little song about the ocean. Something about *when her hair falls into the water it untangles into anemones of shapes. A snare of kelp. A conch. A crown.* Kate has a nice voice.

The Grundle has had it up to here. SECOND STUPID BABY has been antagonizing the dog all afternoon. DUMBASS BABY waves a scented candle at the dog, trying to feed the vanilla bean wax to him. The Grundle lightly whacks baby in the face with a fly-swatter.

*Note: Dumbass baby is actually the same as second stupid baby.

TAKESHI is the name of Kate and The Grundle's dog. He has the body and coloration of a border collie and the head of a redback rabbit.

THE GRUNDLE SAYS

Babysitting makes me so freaking appreciative of a life without children.

KATE SAYS

I see exactly what you mean. I'll bet my sister is in her living room right now, face down in her couch. Hardcore fantasizing about an alternative narrative where pregnancy doesn't exist. Until about two minutes before she has to drive back here and pick these baldies up.

THE GRUNDLE SAYS

Probably masturbating too.

KATE SAYS

Yeah, probably. Gross. Don't talk about my sister that way.

THE GRUNDLE SAYS

I'm being sympathetic. When does she have time for it? Has to be such a disaster down there though. Probably doesn't even resemble mammalian genitals anymore.

KATE SAYS

Oh it's an atrocity alright. I saw it once when she was trying on a bathing suit at Target.

THE GRUNDLE SAYS

What was it like?

KATE SAYS

You remember Kuato in *Total Recall*?

THE GRUNDLE SAYS

The misshapen old man who lives wadded inside his brother's stomach?

KATE SAYS

Yeah pretty much like him. With a more substantial combover. And if a bomb had gone off in his face.

THE GRUNDLE SAYS

Jesus and Mary.

KATE SAYS

Yeah so have some respect. If you had squeezed a couple of babies from your penis you'd be considerably more bedridden.

THE GRUNDLE SAYS

Your sister is so grateful when we offer to babysit. I feel embarrassed for her. I've never met parents who ask for more timeouts from their lives.

KATE SAYS

I don't blame them. Were babies always so stupid or is that a new thing? Why are parents constantly claiming babies are smart?

THE GRUNDLE SAYS

Well when a tiny person falls out of a vagina, gets up, starts mumbling, everyone thinks it's a miracle. I can't deny that it is. Relative to other things that drop out of a human body I suppose babies look bright.

KATE SAYS

They're sort of cute though.

THE GRUNDLE SAYS

Yeah, they're cutie pies alright.

KATE SAYS

Otherwise we'd toss them right in the trash can.

THE GRUNDLE SAYS

That would be a waste. I would feed them to Takeshi.

KATE SAYS

They're cuter than two sea otters holding hands.

THE GRUNDLE SAYS

Cuter than lemurs being tickled.

### KATE SAYS

Cuter than whiskers on a pig.

### THE GRUNDLE SAYS

Cuter than dwarf watermelons.

### KATE SAYS

And maybe they're smarter than we think too.

### THE GRUNDLE SAYS

They're morons. Babies don't get smart until about two hundred and sixteen months.

### KATE SAYS

You mean when they go away to college?

### THE GRUNDLE SAYS

I think they're finally running out of steam. Do you want me to make you a sandwich?

### KATE SAYS

Make me two sandwiches, please.

The Grundle moves into the kitchen and begins peeling and chopping slices of onion atop a cutting board. He sings a song to himself while he chops and cries. *Diamond of the soil. Earth sugar. Witch doctor of my sandwich. Pale ghost-rider. Desert apple. Harvest moon.*

### III.

Kate and The Grundle are in bed, having finished lovemaking. They pass a joint back and forth. Only a thin, damp sheet over their nakedness. Kate's hair spreads over the pillows like black water. One of The Grundle's hands swims alongside like a dark fish. Stuffing protrudes from the corners of their pillows.

### THE GRUNDLE SAYS

I was dreaming for a second. I was dreaming I was in a room filled to the ceiling with your hair. I was pushing my way through it to find you. Your hair was so heavy it made sounds as I moved it.

### KATE SAYS

What kinds of sounds?

### THE GRUNDLE SAYS

Like, a dull crashing. Like water thudding. Salty water.

KATE SAYS

Saltwater. You mean the sea? Waves?

THE GRUNDLE SAYS

Right. Waves crashing. I forgot that word for a second.

KATE SAYS

Did you find me hiding in my hair? What was I doing?

THE GRUNDLE SAYS

I couldn't find you.

KATE SAYS

I was probably in the bathroom.

THE GRUNDLE SAYS

Maybe.

KATE SAYS

What did you do with the condom?

THE GRUNDLE SAYS

In the trashcan.

KATE SAYS

Okay but did you roll it in tissue?

THE GRUNDLE SAYS

Yes.

KATE SAYS

Because we had the ant problem last winter. They will eat anything.

THE GRUNDLE SAYS

I rolled it up good.

KATE SAYS

Fine. I believe you.

Beside Kate there is a bedside table. Atop the table is a hot plate and atop the hot plate a tiny black cauldron. Kate produces a half-loaf of bread, pulls a piece from it, submerges the piece into the cauldron, eats it.

THE GRUNDLE SAYS

How is that cauldron working out?

KATE SAYS

I like eating fondue in bed. It is the only place to truly eat fondue. What did you ask me?

THE GRUNDLE SAYS

I said is that a good cauldron?

KATE SAYS

I'm not sure. Where did you get it?

THE GRUNDLE SAYS

Online.

KATE SAYS

Yeah. It's pretty good.

# THE NORTHEAST

PENNSYLVANIA ▬ THE GREEN MAN
## ROUTE 351

RHODE ISLAND ▸ MERCY BROWN
## EXETER IN RHODE ISLAND, 1892

NEW JERSEY ⚡ THE JERSEY DEVIL & JUNGLE HABITAT
## POPUESSING

MAINE ▲ THE MAINE MYSTERY BEAST
## THE MYSTERY BOX

MASSACHUSETTS ⬛ THE DOVER DEMON
## WHEN YOU'VE SEEN BEYOND

NEW HAMPSHIRE ▲ THE PORTSMOUTH ALIENS
## DO YOU REMEMBER?

# ROUTE 351

## Rachel Lee Taylor

*"This horribly deformed man, also called Charlie No-Face, could be seen at night, blowing cigarette smoke through the holes in his cheek, lurking by the roadside, trying to stay out of sight. It sounds like a classic bogeyman story, except for one detail. It's true. Well, some of it is."*

- Merk Sceurman, *Weird U.S.: The ODDyssey Continues*

First, pink. Then, burgundy. Scarlet. Coral. Cerise.

The Green Man used to walk around here. Ray, to his friends. Charlie-No-Face. There's not much to do in Koppel, anyway. Even if you do still have a face.

Route 18 leads south, six miles to Beaver Falls and north, fourteen miles to New Castle. Do you like kilometers better? Ten, twenty three. Route 351 crosses Route 18 and goes through Koppel, northeast three miles to Ellwood City and west two point five miles to Interstate 376 at the Pennsylvania Turnpike. Five kilometers northeast, four kilometers west.

I like to walk it at night too. What else is there? Koppel, Pennsylvania.

I pick them up along the road. Nighttime is good for that. I like the bus stops, bus stops are good. Outside of bars are good, now that you can't do it inside. Rest stops, truck stops. Bus stops are best, though, because sometimes you can watch them waiting for a little while before you get it. That's good, though, that's the best.

Charlie, Ray, can I call you Ray? I'd like to think so. Ray, we could have shared a cigarette. Not these, of course. Not mine, but a regular one. You would be out walking, and I would be out walking. We could stand by this fence and you could ask, well, not really ask because your tongue is pretty much melted, but I would know what you want and I would give you one. I would light it for you. We could stand on the side of the road together and smoke. I wouldn't ask to take your picture. Maybe you would want to take mine. Haha, Ray.

First, red was my favorite. Red red. Fire engine. The lines crisp, edges sharp and perfect, scarlet on white. I started to notice little differences. Orange red, blue red. Blondes, brunettes. Torch. Brick. Red heads are scared of it. They shouldn't be, I think. Harlot colored. Cherry. Whore red. That's what I liked about it, at first. Lately I've noticed myself becoming more of a romantic. The edges are a little blurry. I've got a fondness for kitten pink. Charmant Coral. Pink Pearl Pop. Its different, but it gets me there.

I found a good one today on Charlie's 351. Sorry, Ray. Ray's 351. It was stubbed out on the ground by the bus stop. Imprinted with a pale, a very pale pink ring. Soft, milky, bright. Revlon, I think. Sky Pink. Silly name, but what do you want for 4.99? Creamy. Kissably soft, but matte, not shiny. Not sparkly. She doesn't need to be a disco ball, she doesn't need everyone to look. I know a lot about them from the mark their lips leave behind. Half of it was left to smoke, more than half, even. The bus must have pulled up just as she was getting into it. She doesn't bite down hard on the filter. I like that. I'll find a quiet place soon, somewhere we can be alone together.

I can't smoke in the house. I wouldn't, anyway, no privacy. No privacy anywhere, but 351 at night is better, better than nothing. Behind the screen of trees at the bus stop is good. Then, sometimes they're there while I'm smoking it and I can see them. That's best. But I don't need it, though, I don't need that to get me there. All I need is the pink lined up with my lips, and I taste them, and I breath smoke, breath through their lips and their breath and their lungs, and my head is bright, light, pink, pink as a cloud in the pink pink sky.

━

I met the girl, Ray. Sky Pink, do you remember? That's her favorite, she wears it a lot, but she can wear whatever she wants. She looks good in every color. Even the dark ones, the purples, the wine darks that can make the lips too small in their pinched faces with their big smudgy eyes. She can be soft too, I can see that. She can be just a whisper, something secret that only I can see. She can be bright. Yesterday she was fire. I could weep. I could die.

She's a beautiful girl. I can't tell you what it is - what would that even mean to you, beautiful. She's the radiator in winter. She's the sun on your face, Ray. Could you still feel it afterwards? I don't know if you could, but then, she's the memory of it for you. Maybe she's how you felt with your face touching the darkness at night. When you could walk at night with your whole self out, unseeing but everyone else unseeing too. I'm not an ugly man, Ray, but I know sometimes the brighter it is the worse everything looks. And I'm afraid. I'm afraid of what I'll look like with everything out in the light for her to see. But I want her to see me too, I want it more than anything for her to see me like I see her, all of her, the good and the bad.

Ray, did you regret trying to save those little birds? Would you have regretted it more if you had left them there on the power lines to die?

◾

We wait for the bus and she dreams; I read the news awhile. She works in town yet, thats why she takes this bus. I've never known a comfortable silence like this. Just stillness, together. You know, its funny how these things start, like, she'll never know how much I thought about her before we met. Of course you know that. I always carry a lighter and it was raining; her matches wouldn't stay lit, one after another they went out, like the weather was helping me say hello. And that was that. I decided to take the route instead of walking now, spend time together. I miss you, Ray. I'm sorry I don't come around anymore. But you understand.

I want to tell her about your birds, Ray, about how I think you're sort of a hero even though you were just a kid and it was really only an accident after all. I think she would understand because she has a soft kind of heart. She would understand about you even though she has a face made for the daytime, made for everyone to look at it and feel better. I think she would because I think she was lonely too, like somehow something beautiful is always lonely because its unique and its rare. But me, I wasn't lonely before, I had everything I needed. I didn't know there was something else I wanted until now. Now when I'm not with her I know what it is to need. All I needed before was the color of their mouths on the cigarettes and myself, but now I don't need any of that, I just need her. I just need the color of her alone. She loves birds too, Ray. She wears a little swallow over her heart, tattooed in lipstick red. Her heart races, it beats its wings.

I loved her so much, just then.

◾

I know it sounds ungrateful, but sometimes I wonder if she really loves me. I mean, really loves me as much as I love her. Sometimes I stay away, to see if she misses me. If she even says anything about it. Is that petty? I don't know. It all seems so confusing sometimes. I look at the side of her face in the sun and I could die, I want her so much, want to breath her in on pink smoke, my lips on hers forever. And sometimes I sit next to her and I feel like she's a hundred miles away. I feel it like ice under my skin, I feel it in my heart crushing itself. Sometimes we don't speak for days.

■

I'd do anything to feel close to her again, like it was in the beginning. She disappears now, for days on end. Its making me crazy, Ray. I don't know why she's acting this way. I don't know what I did to deserve this. She's so cool towards me. I've started to feel like I need something else again, to go off on my own and get myself there, since she's acting this way. So, I've started picking them up again. Its not like I don't love her anymore, I do, I love her as much as I ever did, more even. I just need to do it sometimes, though it's hardly any good anymore. We never talk anymore.

■

She won't even look at me, now. She saw me picking it up. It was pink, so pink, just like the first time, the filter still moist and round. She saw me go to put it in my pocket for later. I just wanted to feel close again. I just needed her again, like it used to be. I needed something. She asked me why, and she had this look on her face like she knew. I lied to her, I said I was going to find an ashtray, somewhere to throw it away. Not that I was mad at her for dropping it on the ground or anything, just that I was going to...she just looked at me, then she looked away and that was all.

■

They don't sell swallows at the pet shop, no red birds at all. All they have are these little blue and yellow ones, but it will have to do. She will love it and everything will be good again. She will know I understand her. She'll forgive me then, for my weakness, and for the things I do, things I can't help but to do. She'll know I love her, still. It wasn't hard to find her house, its close to the stop. I've seen the direction she comes from in the morning and the direction she goes at night. Northeast 351, half a mile at most. I walk the ditch between the road and the trees, like we used to do, Ray, and I feel you with me. I see beautiful ones all around me, cherry, peach, sand, nude, taupe, plum. But I leave them behind, I'm leaving all that behind me now. You give me the strength, having you with me, and she gives me the strength because of her love. I won't need any of that anymore once I have her with me again. She will smile and say hello, come here often, haha, then the quiet, the great soundless love we share as we wait together - so good, the best, the best thing I've ever known.

And so, we'll wait here, together until she gets home, which should be any minute now. I can't think of what I'll say, it's true we've never really had to speak very much, but I think I'll know when the time comes. The cage rocks gently as the not-red bird hops. I don't want to scare her, so I wait a little beyond the trees. I'm glad you're with me.

■

And now I know she didn't understand anything ever, and I didn't understand anything and she never knew me and I never knew her. Not anything about her except
the color of her lips, Christ and that's all I'll ever know now. She doesn't know and
she doesn't care and she never did and she never will. She never cared about me, and
she never cared about you, Ray, she wouldn't have cared about you and your fucking
hideous face and your stupid birds, or why you even went up into the wires for them. I
don't care why you it did anymore either. It was stupid, it was so stupid. You were just
a stupid kid and you ruined your life and for what. You make me want to puke, Ray.
And this thing, Ray, this thing I don't want it. I don't want to take care of it. I don't
want to feed it and watch it and keep it from killing itself. It hurts me to look at it, its
so pathetic. I can't stand it. I can't stand it, I can't Ray, I can't do it, I hate it and it
dies so easy, just anything, you just hold it hard you dig your fingers in and break it
apart you break it into its pieces and it dies. It just dies, Ray. I hated it and I couldn't
help it, it would have died anyway so I just did it. I did it, ok. I did it, Ray, I did it I did
it I did it I'm sorry. I didn't mean to oh god I'm so sorry Ray I'm so sorry.

■

Dear Ray.
Nice to meet you.
You can call me Charlie.
Dear Charlie.
Nice to meet you.
You can call me Ray.
Nice to meet you.
Nice to meet you.
I'm not an ugly man, Ray.
I'm not an ugly man, Charlie.
I know. I know. I'm glad you're with me.
I'm glad you're with me, too.
Its almost dark, Ray.
That it is, Charlie.
Lets go walking.

# EXETER IN RHODE ISLAND, 1892

## Adam Veal

*"Mercy Brown is arguably North America's most famous vampire because she is the most recent. The event caused such a stir in 1892 because newspapers such as the Providence Journal editorialized that the idea of exhuming a body to burn the heart is completely barbaric in those modern times. As Dr. (Michael) Bell said, 'Folklore always has an answer – it may not be a scientifically valid answer, but sometimes it's better to have any answer than none at all'."*

- Jeff Belanger, *World's Most Haunted Places*

The worm which turns the soil gives her the pale skin. In the summer humidity, in the fog, the air somehow both hot and cold, her dress billows. The simple shift she wears with the crumbling earth above the river up the hill. The worm under the fog brushes her stomach which beats with a healthy pulse. She can see the people below on the road by the water. Cemetery Street or Church depending on the north or the south of the square. Cobbled square, cobbled people, they are building a big wooden platform. The ones who don't build, watch. When the platform is finished they bring a man with tied hands and feet shuffling through the crowd. They put him on the platform. He stands alone until a different man with a big broad hat steps up to brush his hair. The people watching embrace one another.

The worm is in the earth and the worm is in the fog. The fog moves like her dress. It swishes this way and that and the worm is in her dress sucking at her pulse. The sun moans on a sick-bed, very soft but very loud. The tied man below in the square is like a fairy tale. He looks like any other person, but the sense of him is upset. He swings one way and then jerks to sway back, like a metronome someone has reset. At the top of the hill she paces back and forth and then stops and realizes that she's been pacing back and forth. She picks up a branch and pretends to trace shapes on the trunk of one of the trees. The tree is creaking in the wind and she cocks her head at one side to listen.

When they want new wool the people will take a sheep. Against the sheep's skin they take the shears so that its skin rolls in their hands. The wool they take and furiously spin. The people bring out a blanket and wrap the tied man in it. When they want wood the people will take a tree. They put the man in a box. They take out his heart and pass the roundness of it between them. They walk up to the hill-top where she swings her legs in the air. The people embrace themselves and bless themselves and she is very cold. She goes down to where they've buried the man and the earth there is warm and soft and the colors of it are all mixed up. She looks up at the people standing around like crows and she watches as they go everywhere.

She turns around at a thick, watery noise. Someone is coming out of the river and she doesn't like how he looks, like a townsperson who's been leftover. If he comes closer she's going to tell him off. The water bubbling out of his mouth. The sogginess of his clothes and his cold fat. So unlike the warmth of the townsfolk now, like the baker and the brewer's wife with their wonderful bellies. The man from the river sees her and tries to speak. He vomits a stomachful of water. She wrinkles her nose and slaps him across his cheek. Some of his teeth come away in her hand. His eyes get big and he crumples into himself. She pushes him over and down and kneads him into the dirt. He flakes all away like curd. She stirs him into the dirt.

On her way back to the town there are five old horses. They are very ill-fed, she can see their ribs, and as she's looking at them they turn to each other and talk about her. She stares at them as she walks by and they stop talking about her when she gets close enough to hear. She keeps walking and they start talking again when she's out of ear-shot. Their whining voices rising and falling. She walks around a bend and the horses disappear behind a grassy hill. There have never been any horses. There is a young boy in the road ahead of her. He is out for his first walk after a brief illness. She bends down and puts him in her hand. He struggles so she squeezes. His blood bursts out of him. She holds him to her mouth and slurps.

She leaves him in the grass, propped up against the fence. There are little thickets everywhere. She hears a noise in one and sees a tangle of bluebirds. She squints until only their color smudges through her lashes. Flashes of blue against the grey green. The air has gotten colder without her noticing. She stares away in a field at the moon, wondering how long the sun has been down, when there is a little clutch of fires on the road. The fires bob along like determined bugs. They stop where the boy sits. She moves close enough to see the people touching their fingers to their hearts and their foreheads. Fingers, hearts, and heads, and a movement in between like turning pages. The man with the big broad hat is there, too. He fidgets a lot, pinching and pulling at his shirt and pants. She likes the hat so she touches its brim; now there are two hats.

An orange-skin and an orange. She peels one hat from him and puts it on her head and leaves the other on him so he doesn't get cold. The people pick up the boy and carry him down the road and after a while she decides to follow.

She remembers that there is a town and that she had wanted to go there. The people must be walking to the town. She's having trouble keeping up with them. The road twists through the hills and their fires get smaller, sometimes disappearing for a bit before showing again. She keeps at it, walking slowly when she needs to, and comes across the boy, standing in the road before her. He is looking at her. She takes off the man's hat and puts it on the boy's head. His brow scrunches up while his lips stay slack. She continues along and after a while looks back. The boy is gone. She hears voices and turns to their source. There are five horses standing on a white dinner plate by a fence post. She asks them if they're the same horses from before, but she can't understand their response. Their mouths are full of bugs. There is a spot in the dirt that might be a shadow, but once she kneels down closer, she sees it is really a shallow smear of blood. She pokes it and sniffs her finger. It smells like the boy.

There are lots of stars but only one moon. She takes that moon and turns it over and puts it on the other side of the sky. Then, she takes each moon in each hand and turns them again and divides the sky into four quadrants, with each quadrant centered around its own moon, and each moon showing a different phase. The worm under the night comes to her and gives her a book. She sits in the grass to read. The story is about a woman, nineteen years. The woman was named after a kind of knife, cold and silver like a fish, that one gave away as a gift. A formal, but sweet thing like a wedding present. The story is about a family dying of a white fever that lets blood escape in coughs. She shuts the book, nonplussed. Why did the father blame the woman for the fever? The knife and fish of the woman's name would never touch him. The worm rests next to her, breathing heavily. She pats the mass of the side of the worm and sends it away.

She notices that she's pacing again. The book has her really wound up, maybe. Is the father in the town? She will go and find him and ask him.

She stands in the center of town. A lot of time must have passed, because it's still night, but she hasn't gotten tired, and so it must be a new night. The town is covered in ice and snow. She wraps her dress around her and looks around. Every house has put in every window a small candle. The glow of each candle comes outside the windows and reflects against the snow. It's not very much light, overall, but it's enough to be pretty and cheerful. She wanders from house to house, looking in each, watching the people for a bit if they're up, before moving along again. She smiles and hums a melody she's inventing as she goes. In one window she sees an older man sitting in a chair, he's coughing into a napkin. She opens the door and walks inside.

First of all, she must be very cold. She takes his jacket, his socks and his shoes, and his pants, too, belting them up under her dress. She takes almost all his clothes and leaves him with them as well so he doesn't get cold. She gets up on his chair and straddles him, digs her hands into his sides above his hips, pulls out what she can grab of his lungs and eats them, tossing her head back as she does. With her forearms flat against his chest, she rubs back and forth while pressing down with her weight, until his ribs crack and break, the sternum caves and she elbows her way in, biting at his liver, his heart, the meat of him, she noses upward to get at the base of his tongue, like a wolf, pulling her head back to swallow and biting forward again, she follows his tongue up inside of his neck, the skin breaking apart on the bridge of her nose, until the muscles of his shoulders constrict, tilting his head back and his jaw open, his eyes on the ceiling, her burrowing into the wet husk of him.

In him there is the worm and the horses. In the dark cave under the earth they all sit around a table. The cave is both the cave and the house where the woman from the book and her family lived. She turns to the horses and asks, Brother and sister and mother, Would you please introduce me to the other two you're with? They grow large and spindly. In growing so their skin and meat stretch on their frames. Like birds they peer at her. She Well-I-Never's them and she How-Rude's them until they shrink back down again. One of the ones she doesn't know gets up and goes to the kitchen to fetch the kettle and cakes. When that one comes back she says, Thank you very much.

The chair is cushy and comfortable and the fire has died down into warm coals. She has curled the older man upon her lap and stretched out beneath him, wrapping her arms around him, a good place to prop her hands. Now, a small group of people stands in the room staring at the older man in her lap. With their fingers they are turning the pages across their chests. She can see them thinking that it is the sickness and also not the sickness. It is both there and not there. The man with the hat is among them. He's taken it off and balanced it on top of the coat rack. He takes a book from his pocket and flips through it. His lips are moving with the book but she can't quite hear the exact words. But he sounds polite and properly formal. He doesn't cajole or order or plead. She gets up and walks over to stand in front of him. She looks at him and she's confused about who's taller, the room seems to pivot. Blue spots appear in her vision. Her stomach turns over and she buckles. She bends over and retches the blood and the meat on the floor. She stands up and brushes herself off and looks around. The stink in the room is of fear and shock. She turns on her heel and walks away. She goes out the back door.

The sun is very hot and close and there is no ice or snow. A lot of time has passed, again. From the back stoop of the house she goes through the town. All the people are dressed lightly, in bright colored clothes. She looks up the hill and sees all the wildflowers blooming. They are all dressed alike, flowers and people. Across from her a young man and a young woman bounce down the road. But there is a strong smell in the air. She looks around and in the eaves of every house hangs a tiny head. The heads

EXETER IN RHODE ISLAND, 1892

are from the plant that grows a long green stalk with a small purple flower on top. She approaches one and smiles, she likes the papery skin of it, likes the pale waxy clove inside. She touches it and it burns her fingers a bit.

With her hands clutched to her breast she goes in every direction at once. She fills up her eyes with the world. Everything is beautiful! She opens her eyes and she is walking down the road. There is the river. There is the worm warning her away from it. An old woman sits alone on a bench, mending some knitting. The old woman smiles at her, Do I know you? I don't think I recognize you. She says, Oh! Yes, I was born here. I come and go.

# POPUESSING

## Anthony Muni Jr.

*"'That's the conundrum, the mystery,' Noah pointed out.
'Around here the Jersey Devil is the explanation for anything
unusual that anybody happens to see.'*

- John Calu, *Mystery of the Jersey Devil*

*"For me, though, there will always be just two Jungle Habitats:
the hot and smelly wild safari park of my youth, and the
abandoned ruin I explored later in life, when things started
getting really weird."*

- Mark Moran and Mark Sceurman, *Weird N.J.*

This moment, in its silence and cold, is a threat to every lonely person. I am ankle deep in snow, collecting firewood from beneath a tarp in my backyard. The subtle malevolence of winter surrounds me from all sides, and I am prepared to retreat, not ashamed to lock myself away. It was fear, after all, which kept me alive.

§

It was 1976 when the animals went feral. They roamed the neighborhood, claws overgrown, fur tangled. They bred with freedom, ate their fill from unguarded trash bins. At night, they chittered and screeched, the haunting sounds echoed through tree lines until morning traffic rolled across town and the ghouls vanished into the hills. As time passed, the streets were strewn with the rotting guts of peacocks and other foreign bodies. Some days, the wind would shift, and families down the hill were hit with the unfamiliar stench, forcing them to evacuate. Outraged residents banded together to hunt the intruders, the gunfire could be heard well into the night. The newspaper spent weeks reporting ghastly and unfortunate events; domestic pets torn apart by wolves, baboons ransacking the local pharmacy, carcasses bloating in a clearing near the safari park from which others had escaped.

§

On opening day, Jungle Habitat created a traffic jam 28 miles long. Families from across the tri-state area sat in their overheated cars, heaving from sun stroke. Advertisements for the park offered visitors an afternoon of adventure, where exotic creatures such as lions, zebras, and elephants, roamed free. Although the park was profitable in its early years, it suffered the slings of poor publicity following an incident the first summer, wherein a man by the name of Abraham Levy taunted a pair of lions with a slab of meat. Paka, the alpha male, mauled the man through the window, causing lacerations across the arm and shoulder. Amongst the media melee, it was also discovered that several creatures contracted tuberculosis and were euthanized. Following Halloween weekend, 1976, the park closed its doors.

*

The animals were abandoned. The sick and infirm were feasted upon or left to die. An elephant lay dead in its cage,its bones picked clean by carrion and larger beasts. Lions and wolves made their homes in the mountains, while apes and birds nestled in the boughs of oak trees. The home evacuations began when the stench of death, which lingered on the wind, became unbearable. And when the world took a breath and became silent, the shrieks of baboons could be heard from the forest.

*

I dreamed of an eternal chase, some strange and dangerous creature on my heels, until at last, I missed a step, and it pinned me to the ground. The claws overgrown, the skin separating with ease, the phantom ate its fill.

*

I took a shortcut through a well beaten path. The field running alongside me was bare of trees or brush, and would have been a pure, white eye on the back of the earth, had it not been for the heaving outline of Paka as he ripped into the belly of a freshly slain deer. The simplicity of white was complicated with red. Then, without warning, came a deafening shriek,the violent snapping of branches introduced another creature into the clearing. Its leathery wings unfurled like the canvas of an old cargo ship. Paka climbed to his feet, but his motions were slowed by the weight of his kill. I stood, unflinching, as the beast tore into Paka's throat.

*

Now, this moment, in its silence and cold, is the least of my concerns, as there comes a screech in the night, an unholy sound. There comes a screech and it tears the fabric of the universe, it does well to camouflage itself in the trees. I am unprepared to re-treat as I am unsure in which direction to run. The back door is open, and the safety of home is within reach, still I am a statue in ankle deep snow, paralyzed. Twigs snap be-neath the weight of some unseen assailant, its breath plumes, then disappears, plumes, then disappears. Beneath my feet comes the rhythmic thumping of Paka's long silent heart, and through a trickle of stale moonlight, the eternal chase comes to a close, I am on my back, and the simplicity of white is complicated by red.

# THE MYSTERY BOX

## Sunny Katz

*"After the second night's attack, neighbors woke to find carcasses scattered across their yards, a tough thing to swallow when you think that all you're heading for is your first cup of coffee and the newspaper... As far as central Maine is concerned, the beast is still out there."*

- Michelle Souliere, *Strange Maine*

The bucket seats of my '91 Oldsmobile Cutlass Supreme are thick with self-loathing. Echoes of laughter from eighty-three faceless studio audience members play over and over in my mind as I try to stay focused on the road. Warm soda spills all over my jeans and I officially hate myself.

"FUCK YOU, MYSTERY BOX!" I scream at the empty cardboard receptacle covered in question marks.

Jasmine is waiting for me in our kitchen, her eyes glittering in anticipation to hear how I did.

She looks at the Mystery Box.

Our eyes meet.

She looks at the Mystery Box.

Our eyes meet.

She opens her mouth and takes a breath.

"Nope, no way, Jasmine. You already know what happened," I say with all the enthusiasm of a corpse.

"But—"

"I'M NOT TALKING ABOUT THE MYSTERY BOX, JAY!"

Jasmine falls silent and I know she is thinking about how she spent the last two days prepping me for *Let's Forge a Transaction*, our town's shitty knock off version of *Let's Make a Deal*. She'd signed me up for the show months ago as an April Fool's prank, but since then we'd both gotten weirdly excited about my future game show stardom. As we'd drilled on how I would play, every lesson in strategy ended with a firm admonishment to never, under any circumstances, pick the Mystery Box.

*Transaction*'s version of the Mystery Box had become a running joke on our local news—if it had ever been picked, no one could remember when. In the studio it was evident the Box was covered with dust and grime.

But as I'd stood under the flourescent lights, my fate became entwined with the Mystery Box. Every deal I made went bad. Every trade was worse. By the time I leave the studio that night, the Box is mine.

The Mystery Box earns of a place of distinction in my closet. It nestles next to a few "honorable mention" trophies, a jar of name tags, and my most recent publication rejection letter. As I store it away, I notice that it's heavier than an empty box should be.

That night I fall into a restless sleep and dream only in shadows.

*"Wake up."*

I turn over.

*"Wake up."*

I turn over.

*"Wake up, **now**."*

My eyes open and adjust to the dim early morning light.

My room is silent.

Everything is fine.

I lay back down.

Everything is fine.

The closet door is open. The Mystery Box is open.

Everything is fine.

Wait. What?

*"Do you still believe everything is fine?"*

The voice is low, guttural.

"...Yes?"

My sympathetic nervous system is making a very compelling argument to try my luck with escaping out my third story window. Modern medicine is quite wondrous and I would probably be put mostly back together again.

*"You would never make it."* Its tone drips with venom, blood, and other assorted unpleasant liquids.

Oh my fuck, where is that...*thing*?

*"Look up, stupid."*

Don't look, don't look, don't look.

I look.

A canine giving zero fucks about the law of gravity sits on my ceiling. It's coat is jet black, vaguely reflective, and I kind of want to pet it even though the primal part of my brain identifies that desire as "very bad". The creature has two pools of white for eyes which I file under "unsettling". Its mouth opens to reveal row after endless row of perfect little razor sharp triangular teeth.

Wait.

No, it can't be.

There is no way it has a snake for a tongue because that doesn't seem scientifically possible. Not to mention that it is super gross.

*"My* tongue *is the one thing about this whole situation you find the most difficult to be-lieve? Really?"* The Beast asks while cocking its head.

"Well, yeah. I mean, is it a separate creature or does it only function as your tongue? Follow up question, if it exists independently that suggests it would have to eat, which leads me to wonder how and more importantly *where* does it poop?? Further—"

*"Silence, worm! Your pseudo-science talk offends me."*

I shut up because it seems like a very good idea and I prefer to not see that horrific tongue up close.

*"You woke me from my eternal slumber. You, who are a sniveling pile of filth. You, who are not fit to even lick the floor I step on."*

"Question. Does sleep still count as eternal if you can wake up from it?"

The Beast raises up on all fours and howls.

*"You open your mouth and spew garbage. I would ask if you even bother to think before you think, but your thoughts are even worse. Old Gods, do you even know what a blight it is to hear the words and contemplation from someone like you?"* the Beast spits.

"Well, yeah, of course I do," I say.

The Beast twists its body and descends from the ceiling. It lands lightly on my bed and leans in close.

*"I am going to enjoy watching you suffer. I am going to revel in every moment as you scream for mercy. Your anguish will be my revenge."*

"Sounds like someone needs a belly rub."

*"Open wide, fool."*

"Wait, I—"

The Beast folds into itself and claws it's way into my mouth. I am thrown onto my back, choking, sputtering, trying to scream. My eyes roll back into my head, I convulse, and am enveloped into nothing.

♠

*Morning comes and goes. The body of the woman rises, looks over her hands. This is going to be fun. Deep inside, the consciousness of the woman who once was stirs and pulls against her chains. She tries to speak, tries to stop her former body from moving, tries to make a sound.*

*She is met with nothing.*

*She is nothing.*

*She can only watch.*

*The body of the woman stands and moves towards the sound of water running. Prey always make so much noise when they don't know they're being stalked.*

*The door opens easily. The woman ignores the indignant questions of the occupant because they are irrelevant. Her arms strike with alarming speed and hands like serpents wrap around the soon-to-be dead human's neck. Her quarry struggles, increasing the thrill. Her grip tightens and the once strong protests are reduced to winces. The woman inclines her head. It's best to watch life leave up close. One last shuddering inhale and it is done.*

*The woman tosses the body aside, looks into the mirror. She smiles.*

"I am going to kill everyone you have ever loved. I am going to rip them apart while wearing your skin. When I am through, you are coming with me and you will beg for death."

*Her tongue darts out like a viper, licking the back of her hand.*

"Never, under any circumstances, pick the Mystery Box."

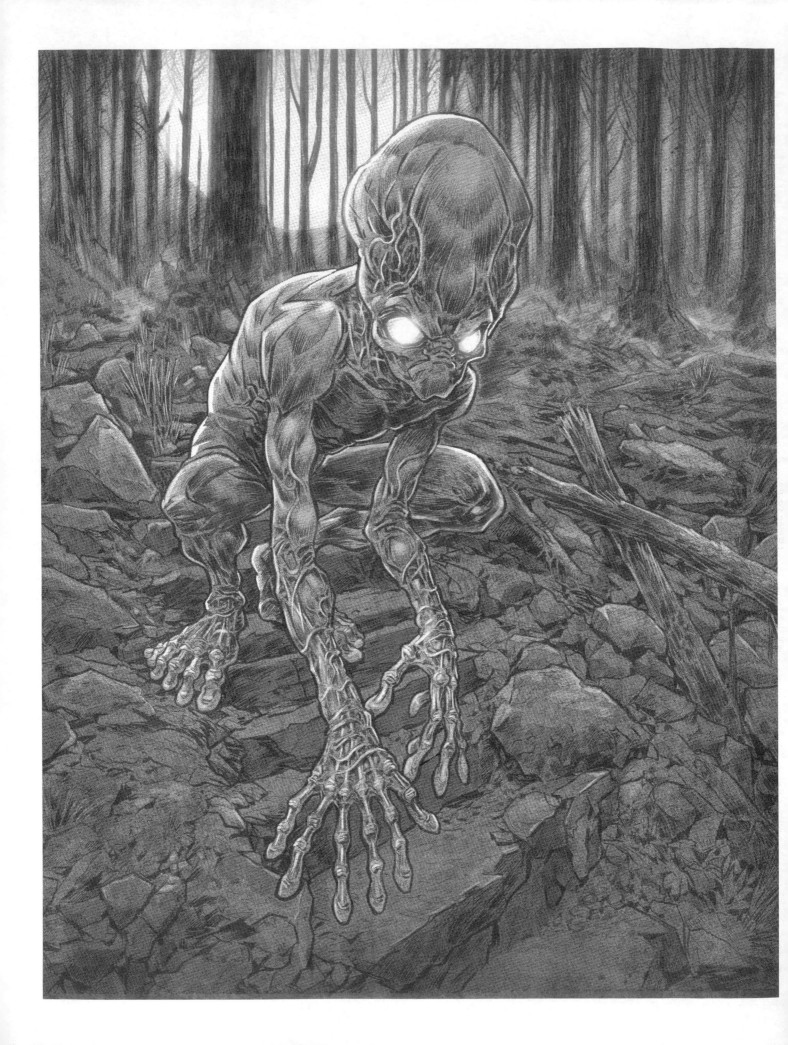

# When You've Seen Beyond

## Ed Farragut

*"Three separate sightings unfolded quietly in April 1977 in the rural community of Dover, a town with more horses than people. The witnesses described a small, extremely thin, four-foot-tall creature. It had a disproportionately large, figure-of-eight-shaped head and spindly fingers. While there was a general agreement of the bright orange color of the hairless body and its sand-paper-texture skin, there was a difference of opinion of the color of its eyes. However, the witnesses were unknown to each other and described essentially the same thing, independently, to all the investigators involved."*

- Loren Coleman, *Mothman and Other Curious Encounters*

She's so cool. All gum chewing bad-assery, torn hoodie, and watching the *Saw* movies like it's no big deal. Casey is the most awesome best friend a 12-year-old girl could ask for.

The older girl is so close to us we can smell her Colgate. "What'd you just say?" she asks.

I don't know these girls but they know me and they don't like me. My mom is the new Assistant Principal at their reform school. Mom made them wear their ties and that was enough to make them come down on me. I take a step back.

Casey doesn't. A small, tight pink bubble expands from her lips. She pinches it off with her teeth, pulls it back in her mouth, and snaps it like a dry twigs. "I think I called you a bad word," she says.

"You did," the older girl says. "You called me a very bad word. That's not nice."

Casey shrugs. "You were being mean to my friend, even though she didn't do anything. Her name's Jane. She likes comics books and has cool sneakers. So you should be nice to her. If you're not nice, you get called bad words."

This is the first time Casey has called me her friend. And she thinks my red Vans with the Flash logo I drew on them are cool. Even though we're both about to get our butts kicked: best day ever.

The older girl laughs. "Comics are for boys," she says. "Are you two boys?"

"Comics are for awesome people," Casey says.

The older girl laughs again. Casey pushes the wad of pink gum into the corner of her mouth, swelling her lower lip. "Comics," the older girl starts, "are for—"

Casey's fist retracts from the girl's stomach as sharp and hard as it landed. The older girl doubles over and Casey spins on her heels, looks at me, and we take off.

We run as fast as we can, as fast as my Flash shoes can carry me. Casey's taller and I have to pump my legs twice as much to keep up.

We're halfway down the street by the time we hear the older girl and her friends scream after us. We keep running until we hit the opening in the chain link fence that leads to the Noanet Woodlands.

"C'mon," Casey says as we duck off the path, scrambling through the fallen leaves and dead trees.

We keep moving until the shadows start to resemble jail cell bars, the temperature drops, and the sweat on our brows is salty and cold. We finally stop, panting and gulping air.

"Shit," Casey says. Her head swivels in every direction. I'm new in town, but I recognize her look—that panicked-child look that notices every tree is identical, that the sun is setting faster than we thought.

Noanet Woodlands swallows us and nothing looks like the path home.

The first  drop falls heavy on my face. Then another. A third smacks against the few leaves still clinging to the trees. The rest—giant drops escaping the gray clouds— rhythmically soak everything.

The rain pelts my North Face jacket. Casey pulls her hoodie up and tugs the draw-strings closed. My hair falls in dirty brown streaks over my face. My red Flash Vans feel heavy and tight.

I hear Casey, still chewing that gum that must be a flavorless lump, and I want to cry, but don't.

I don't know if he is psychic or not. But I know that I heard his voice in my head long before I ever saw him.

*"Lost girl,"* hisses in my brain, sharp and clear. A voice that isn't mine. A voice that isn't scared.

I stop walking. The rain grows louder, pounding and slapping against the wet ground, thumping off the branches, but I hear his voice above all. *"Lost girl, needs to go home."*

To Casey, here is what the next ten minutes look like: we walk through the night, through the storm. Then I fall. I'm out for a minute or so. When I wake up, I know the way home. My mom gives us warm towels and hot chocolate. A happy ending.

I don't tell her about the deal until we're older.

Here's what the next 10 minutes look like to me: he doesn't step out from the treeline; he slithers from.

All the kids in town, even the new ones, know about The Dover Demon.

The kids always talk about his mouth with its three rows of razor sharp fangs permanently stained red with blood.

But he doesn't have teeth. He doesn't have a mouth at all. Underneath his enormous, oval, jet-black eyes is smooth, taut skin.

Yet I hear his voice again, that hiss, in my head. *"Are you frightened?"*

I nod, relieved that someone, something, anything is here to save us.

*"I will help you,"* he hisses, *"for a price."*

I nod again.

*"You accept?"* he asks.

"Please just help us."

The Demon fades, as if absorbed by the night.

*"Thank you,"* he hisses. I feel pressure build behind my eyes: as though someone had stuffed a moment of pure midnight in my brain. I forget everything, even words and how to breathe. So I fall among the wet, dirty leaves.

That night, I have the first nightmare.

Four years later, as the clown drops the last shovelful of dirt on my coffin, as I scrape and tear at the lid, as the millipedes burrow into my ear and puncture through the drum, as my third grade teacher dislocates my toes with pliers and sings "A Day In The Life", I wake up and catch the scream in my throat.

I'm an expert at making sure Mom doesn't hear my night terrors. It feels like I'm going to vomit, my whole diaphragm tenses like a dry heave. So I smother my face in three pillows let it out, the blood-curdling pierce reduced to a dull moan. I grab the towel I keep on my desk chair and wipe the sweat from my face. I check to see if I wet the bed again. I didn't. Lucky.

The red numbers glow "4:46". I do the math. 3 hours and 14 minutes of sleep.

I dig under my bed, pull out the old shoebox, and grab a 5-hour energy shot. I only have three bottles left which means another trip to 7/11. At least they sell them in six packs now.

I can't tell if my body is building up a tolerance to the caffeine, but it's all I can do.

I haven't slept peacefully in four years.

Around 15, Casey hit the genetic lottery. She grew six inches and became the most-sought-after Sophomore by every coach. She chose softball. She says its for the cardio, but I know it's because she gets a power trip while at bat.

She shoulders her bulky bag of equipment, all strange protrusions and jutting corners, like a pro. She tosses it in the trunk with ease.

Before she slides into the passenger seat, her eyes fall on the cup holder. "Dude, seriously?"

My turbo Starbucks with two Americano shots is practically the size of the gear shift. "It... it's not mine?" I say.

"You know how bad that is for you? Stunts your growth like there's no tomorrow. You want to be 5'1" your entire life?"

"Can't all be secret super-star athletes." I twist the key and the engine rumbles to life. "Does your mom know that her little nerd-girl is all grown up and about to take MVP?"

"Ugh." Casey folds a long leg up up to her chest and props her feet on the dash. "Don't even joke about that. She'll probably want me to train for the Boston Marathon with her. Let her think I'm lazy."

"Yeah, all the lazy-asses I know can chuck a 70 mile-per-hour fastball."

Casey smiles. "74, dude. Coach clocked me today. I got heat." She squirts a mouthful of water and swallows. "Anyhoo, lady. We gotta talk."

The car slides into traffic. "About what?"

"Uh, fuckin' prom, dude. What do you think?" she says.

I sigh and shake my head. "Do you know what a scapegoat is?"

"That has what to do with what?" Casey asks.

"No, I'm trying to explain," I say. "Okay, so, I'm not entirely sure about all this, but I looked it up. Scapegoating comes from the Bible, when priests would symbolically lay the sins of the people upon an actual goat and then cast it out into the desert."

"So... you're a scapegoat?" Casey asks.

"Worse." I turn the car left instead of right. "I'm the scapegoat's scapegoat."

We're in the 7/11 parking lot and when I tell her everything.

"Do you remember that night in the woods? That night we got lost?" I ask.

Jane looks out the window. "Yeah, we were... what? 12? And that fat-ass Mitzy said we were boys because we liked comic books or whatever?"

"And you punched her, so we ran."

"Punch?" The corner of Casey's mouth curls up. "That doesn't sound like me."

"Oh, you don't remember that?"

"I don't punch, Janey. I administer appropriate proportional physical reactions to people who deserve it. Like Batman." Casey leans across the cupholder and puts her head on my shoulder. "You know I got your back, kid."

And so help me, I start to cry. I can't help it. "You're so brave, Casey. I was always jealous of that. Even that night, in Noanet Woodlands, I was terrified and I remember you wore that hoodie, that blue one, and I kept staring at it, hoping you knew the way home. But you didn't. Neither of us did. So we kept walking, all cold and wet and miserable and hungry. And..."

"Hey," Casey says. "It's cool. You saved us remember? You found the way home."

I inhale and let out a deep breath. "No. No I didn't. He did."

Casey cocks her head and her eyebrows migrate towards the bridge of her knows. "What are you talking about?"

I sigh. "This is where you think I'm crazy," I say. "This is where all the doctors and therapists and sleep disorder specialists stopped believing me."

"Jane, what are you even—?"

"Him," I say. "The Dover Demon. This emaciated, gray-skinned thing with a straight-up Close Encounters alien head and huge black eyes, like the size of mutant cockroaches. And no mouth. The people of Dover created him without knowing and gave him their worst fears, okay? Like the most fucked-up shit they've got nesting in there. And he doesn't have a mouth, so he couldn't scream and he was in pain. So he made a deal with me. He'd get us home, in exchange for..." I stop when I see Casey's mouth. She looks the way they all looked. And I choke back my tears, the tears that come when your best friend is about to call it quits.

I should've known better. Because Casey is the coolest.

"In exchange for the dreams," she says. "You have The Dover Demon's nightmares crammed in your noggin."

I almost start crying again, except big sloppy joyous tears. For the first time, someone believes me.

"Well..." Casey says, biting her lower lip. "That's some horsehit."

The chains around my ankle cuts into the flesh and the rats gnawing at my exposed spinal cord are two bites away from severing it completely. I fumble at the padlock, but the dial wears used hypodermic needles like a crown. The walls are coated with excrement and a baby with a missing jaw is playing with a loaded revolver. "For The Benefit Of Mr. Kite" reverberates down the hall.

I fall out of my blue plastic chair and flail, still trying to figure out the combination to the lock. Casey wrestles my hands, prying them away from my ankle.

Ms. De La Vega is not impressed. A few students snicker. Casey gently lifts me off the scratchy carpet.

"Dude," Casey says, her eyes wide.

Parts of the flesh are torn open on my red, raw ankle. Blood oozes from one of the deeper scratches, where the padlock was.

We're in the nurse's offce when Casey tells me her plan. "I mean, if we went back, back to Noanet Woodlands... you could find him again, right? Like, we were both in the woods that night, right? The Demon should've split the load, given me some of the dreams. But he didn't. Let's re-negotiate. We're just asking for what's fair. It'll be like a really awful timeshare."

"Case, I don't know. I couldn't ask that of you."

Casey lifts my bandaged ankle, "Jane. Get real. Get the car. We're going Demon hunting."

The woods are darker than I remember—all inky blackness and skeletal branches.

"Here take this," Casey says. She hands me a netted bag full of thick yellow softballs. "Maybe you can use it as a mace or something."

"Christ," I say. "He's not a minotaur. Last I saw him he looked like an alien with terminal cancer."

"Jane, we're about to be a couple of geniuses and walk around some weird-ass woods at night. Take the thing, okay?" Jane drops her equipment bag back into the trunk. She unzips it and takes out a black bat with the word "Easton" on it, which she has modified to say "Eastwood." "I'll take Clint."

I feel like I should warn her, tell her that the dreams aren't just bad, they're like a knife to the brain, they bleed and pierce and you wake up hot and sweaty and sometimes vomiting because you can't believe the infectious worm that is crawling around in there making you see terrible imagery of torture, murder, disease. But the worst part is the helplessness. You can never escape.

We walk the same way we did when we were girls—side by side, picking a direction and trying our luck.

Noanet Woodlands swallows us again. The hiss creeps into my brain, like TV static.

"He's here," I say. "We're close."

The first vision hits me hard. A dog. First one then many. All the neighborhood dogs, stalking the streets, every single one of them overthrowing their human masters, hell-bent on ripping their throats asunder. I drop, my knees submerging in the wet mud.

Casey catches me. She pulls me to my feet when the next one hits, knocking me down again.

Broken fingernails. New dress. Eyeballs. Dumpster.

They're coming faster and faster now. I scream. Casey shakes me, but that just turns my brain into nightmare Boggle.

Rope. Doctors. Peanut butter. Global warming. Mud-witches.

"He's here," I manage to say.

Drowning. Genocide. Spiders laying eggs in people's throats.

And then they stop. My head is pounding. I'm not sure if I'm still dreaming when I see him.

The Dover Demon doesn't have a mouth. But I can tell he's laughing at me.

"Jesus," Casey says.

"*Jane,*" the hiss says. "*We had a deal.*"

"I know, but I thought... that is we thought... that maybe we both could—"

*"Leave now!"* he hisses and an image of a baby doll stuffing an emaciated corpse into an oven explodes in my brain.

I start to cry, ashamed and frustrated. "He says no," I squeak.

Casey smiles. "Cool."

She pulls me up, grabbing the netted bag.

Casey holds up a softball, thick and heavy, and shrugs. "Appropriate proportional physical reaction?"

I smile. "Like Batman."

She's so amazingly, wonderfully, cool.

Not sure if it clocks in at 74 miles-per-hour, but the first pitch strikes him between the eyes. The hiss dulls slightly. She winds up and unleashes the second. It smacks the top of his bulbous head, splitting it. A great rivulet of crimson streams across his black eyes. The third explodes into his socket with a hard crack. The mutant cockroach eye dangles by a nerve.

We stand around his bleeding, frail body and Casey hands me Clint Eastwood. The brain-hiss has become a whisper, repeating the same word over and over: *"Sorry..."*

After the final blow, after his gray matter spills and splatters chunks from his over-sized cranium, everything in my head goes quiet.

We walk home, sure of the way.

# Do You Remember?

## Nate MacDonald

Do you remember
eyes pushed into my eyes?
closed my eyes?
walked with them into the woods?

Do you remember
maybe it was the moon?
beacon disappeared at the right time?
ball of fire in the road?

Do you remember
wore black hats?
wraparound eyes?
mumbled?

Do you remember
touched my body?
beeps and coded buzzing?
didn't shock like you expected?

Do you remember
decided not to throw away the dress?
tore my binocular strap?
watches never worked again?

Do you remember the compass's needle, skittering in the air above our car, concentric
circles rubbed through the paint of the roof, the metal
beneath charged?

Do you remember
all I see are these eyes?
cut a piece of your hair?
touched your hands?

Do you remember
shouldn't remember?
changed their minds?
wouldn't let us?

Do you remember
car was on the road though we had driven it into the woods?
three missing hours?
followed us through the mountains?

Do you remember
in the air above the diner?
watched us through the windows?

Do you remember eyes?

Do you remember what happened that night?

Do you remember eyes pushed into my eyes?

# WORDS OF TERROR

RYAN BRADFORD is the founder and editor of *Black Candies*, a literary horror journal. His writing has appeared in *Quarterly West*, *Paper Darts*, *Vice*, *Monkeybicycle*, *Hobart* and *[PANK]*. His novel *Horror Business* is forthcoming from Month9Books.

JULIA DIXON EVANS is a writer in San Diego. Her work has appeared in *Hobart*, *Black Candies*, and in SSWA storytelling shows. She teaches creative writing sometimes. Follow @juliadixonevans

PEPE ROJO writes in Mexican and English as there is no other way to go at it in Tijuana, where he has spent most of his life for the past 8 years. He has published 4 books in Mexican, and directed several interventions and collective imagination experiments in Mexico City and TJ.

JIMMY CALLAWAY lives in San Diego, CA. He tells jokes and does some other stuff. His novel, *Lupo Danish Never Has Nightmares*, will be available from Crime Factory in 2015.

MATT LEWIS is a writer and the editor of *The Radvocate*, a literary arts magazine, and a producer for the non-profit So Say We All. He graduated from Cal State San Marcos with a BA in Literature & Writing in 2009. He lives and eats burritos in San Diego, California.

KEITH McCLEARY is the author of the graphic novels *Killing Tree Quarterly* and *Top of the Heap*, and the audio novella *The Gothickers*, written with Sophia Starmack. His work has appeared in *Heavy Metal*, *Weave*, *theNewerYork*, *Pseudopod*, and comics from Terminal Press. He holds an MFA from UC San Diego.

JESSICA HILT is from a tiny river town in Ohio. She graduated from UCSD and the Clarion Writers' Workshop. Her work can be seen at Bourbon Penn, on stage at the Old Globe, and with So Say We All. When she's not writing, she works as a geek socialite.

HANNA TAWATER received her MFA in Cross-Genre Writing at UCSD. She is the mother of a corn snake named Sue, and in her free time doubles as an elf street samurai in Seattle 2076. Her work can be found in *White Stag*, *The Radvocate*, *New Delta Review*, and *Jupiter 88*.

TINA HYLAND's work has appeared in *BESTIARY: the best of the inaugural demi-decade of A Capella Zoo*, *theNewerYork*, *decomP*, and other print and online journals. She tweets @AnnaNimh.

ALEX BOSWORTH began writing fiction in elementary school and has kept at it for forty years in lieu of gainful employment. His work has been influenced by Kurt Vonnegut and Spalding Gray. His collection of short stories, *Chip Chip Chaw: Tales of the Unsane* is available from Renegade Muses.

JIM RULAND is the author of *Forest of Fortune*, *Big Lonesome*, and co-author with Scott Campbell, Jr. of *Giving the Finger*. He writes for San Diego CityBeat, the LA Times and Razorcake, and has appeared in *The Believer*, *Esquire*, *Granta*, *Hobart* and *Oxford American Magazine*. He also runs the Vermin on the Mount reading series.

KIIK A.K.'s work has been translated into sixteen languages. Kiik performed the translations even though he's never learned another language and is mildly illiterate in English. The translations are conjectures of Kiik if he was Swedish or Chinese, etc. As a result the Swedish and Chinese work is very clever.

RACHEL LEE TAYLOR yearns for you tragically.

ADAM VEAL lives and works in San Diego. He received his MFA in Poetry from Brown University in 2010. His poems have been published in *Lit*, *SpringGun*, and most recently in The Organism for Poetic Research's *PELT*.

ANTHONY MUNI JR. is the author of three books including *Honestly I'm Fine*, *The Seventy-Nine Series*, and most recently, *Sacred Geometry*, all of which can be found online through Lulu Press.

SUNNY KATZ is a fucking cyborg.

ED FARRAGUT studied creative writing at San Francisco State University. His work has appeared in *Black Candies*, he regularly performs non-fiction pieces with the VAMP storytelling showcase, and he co-created the webcomic *Cryptozoo*. He loves comic books and cartoons, because, although 28, he stopped maturing around 14.

NATE MacDONALD left school when it became clear he wouldn't be finishing his Theatre Arts degree. He now writes horror flash fiction about advertising and technology under the name ActualPerson084. Read in sequence, the first letter of each of his tweets spell "HELP" over and over again.

BEN SEGAL is the author of *Pool Party Trap Loop* (forthcoming), *78 Stories*, co-author of *The Wes Letters*, and co-editor of *The Official Catalog of the Library of Potential Literature*. His work has been published by *Tin House*, *Tarpaulin Sky*, *Gigantic*, *Puerto del Sol*, and others. He lives in Los Angeles.

# ART OF TERROR

**ADAM MILLER** is a gallery director and professional art guy. Clients include Budweiser, Nuclear Blast Records and Montserrat College of Art. His work has received recognition from G4TV, The New York Times, *Fangoria* and MSNBC. He writes, teaches, speaks, paints and photographs his way through the art world. *facebook.com/millerstrations*

**JACOB CARIGNAN** creates photorealistic drawings of twisted reality using graphite on paper and stained canvas. He also portrays emotions and characters through abstract and surreal cartoon styles.

**MARLENE N. O'CONNOR** from Lynn, MA, now lives in Brattleboro, VT. She has been making art since childhood, which at this point is a long time. Past work is included in the comics anthology *Taboo*. She works as a graphic designer and illustrator, and on her own paintings and drawings. *marleneoconnorart.com*

**JOSH MORRISSETTE** is a photo-based illustrator from Massachusetts. He has an affinity for building atmospheric scenes that delve in and out of the bounds of reality and photographic ideals. His work has been exhibited throughout New England and in several publications. *facebook.com/jomoillphoto*, @JMIphoto

**JOE DELLAGATTA** is a freelance illustrator from a city just north of Boston. He is currently working on his own book *The Diver*, and probably drinking scotch. *coppercollarillustration@hotmail.com*

**JOHN CARDINAL** is the publisher at Tryptic Press and has a BFA from Montserrat in Illustration. He uses the alias "MONSTA" because it makes him feel like a superhero. To see more of his personal work check out *monstaville.com*, and for all things Tryptic go to *trypticpress.com*.

**THE WIZARD GARRETT** is a gentleman-raconteur, an artist, and a leader of secret rites. His fine art prints are a meditation in magikal application. He found a natural home for his art as a tattoo artist, and through his work he helps people to dance anew in their own flesh.

**ANDREW MACLEAN** is a Salem, MA-based comic creator. He has worked for Dark Horse Comics, Image Comics, NoBrow Press, etc. Andrew is the creator of *Head Lopper*, *SNIP SNIP*, and *ApocalyptiGirl* (Dark Horse 2015), and has lent his art to *KINO* (Lion Forge) and *Department O* (Monkey Pipe).

**DAVID FERREIRA** is an award-winning illustrator working for clients in the advertising, publishing and editorial markets. David has recently created illustrations for Unilever, Hasbro, BacardiUSA, Heineken and ESPN. David is also a passionate teacher, and instructs illustration, painting and drawing courses for colleges, museums and art organizations throughout New England.

**HAIG DEMARJIAN**'s work spans many media. In addition to painting, printmaking and drawing he also co-masterminded the award-winning film *Die You Zombie Bastards!* He writes and draws his comic book *Super Inga*, available at SuperIngaSaga.com. He's a Professor of Art + Design at Salem State University. See more at *artofHaig.com*.

**ANDREW HOULE** is a painter, illustrator and publisher. He has had a busy year making smaller compact oil paintings and hoping Danny Ainge can put it all back together again. He shares a home north of Boston with his wife Melissa, Mila the cat & his comic book collection. *andrewhoule.com*

**ROLO LEDESMA** is an Eisner-nominated artist from New York City. He has done illustration and storyboarding for music videos, comics from Terminal Press, and video games such as *Batman: Arkham City* and *Techno Kitten Adventure*. He is also the co-creator of the comic book series *Curves & Bullets. facebook.com/curvesandbullets*

**ALEX SCHINAS** is a man with unfinished business. Actually, never finishing is his thing, which is why it's amazing he has 3 businesses. The last two things he's finished were conceiving his son, Julian and this piece of art. And truth be told, that's not even finished. Not even close.

**KEVIN ILACQUA** is a nomad of the New England area now residing in Maine. He is an illustrator/printmaker with a flair for all things beautiful and nerdy, yet refined. With an Illustration degree from Montserrat College of Art, Kevin has shown work in Boston and along the North Shore area.

**MICHAEL CROCKETT** is an artist and designer living and working in Boston, MA. Most recently he has been the lead designer for Tryptic Press' annual art anthology, *CHROMA: A New England Art Awakening*. Music, comics, book covers or events; find out what he's working on next at *www.hazeleyesstudio.com*

**BRIAN PATURZO** is a representational artist who depicts people and places surrounding him to reflect the moods and perspectives within. Projects include work published by Terminal Press and Zombastic Productions. Recently his art has shown at The Armory in New Haven, CT and at Visionspace Gallery in Lynn, MA. *brianpaturzo.com*

**DEREK HART** burst from the womb with a crayon in his hand and now primarily works in charcoal, pastels and acrylic paint. He graduated from Montserrat College of Art with a degree in Illustration and currently resides north of Boston, where he is rarely seen outside his dungeon studio. *Derekhartstudios.com*

**BRETT MASON** graduated from Monserrat College of Art in 2012. Mason specializes in contemporary portraiture, abstract paintings and live drawings with two different musical projects. Currently, Mason is the Treasurer of the Beverly Cultural Council and is working on a mural for the city of Beverly, MA.

**MIKE DOHERTY** is an artist–teacher who loves monsters and drawing them is his earliest art memory. Saturday afternoon monster movies were and are the best thing in the world. This is a legacy he is passing on to his kids. He is raising them right. Creature Double Feature rules.

**CHRISTOPHER JAMES LETARTE** is an artist from Whalom, MA. He holds a BFA from Montserrat College of Art. Running his company, Whalom Painting and Woodcraft from his home studio he fulfills commissions for larger scale carvings created primarily with chainsaw. He has shown in galleries in illustration, sculpture and photography.

**STEVE BECKER** is a professional illustrator, graphic designer and most notably art director for an anthology series of *New York Times*-bestselling graphic novels through FUBAR Press. steveabecker@hotmail.com, *steveabecker.wordpress.com*, INSTAGRAM: steveabecker_killustrator

**GREG MOUTAFIS** is a comic book illustrator/designer and an alumni of the Massachusetts College of Art & Design. His parents may or may not have been abducted by aliens on the backroads of New England during the 1960s. Follow Greg's artistic shenanigans at *ComicArtGreg.com*

**EMILY DUMAS** is an illustrator and designer from the Boston area. After beginning in advertising, she left to freelance, teach and run her stationery company Flowers in May. She has been published in blogs, showcased her work in galleries and licensed her illustrations. Her work can be seen at *flowersinmay.com*

# RESEARCH OF TERROR

Beatty, Judith S. and Lamb, Denise M. La Llorona: Encounters with the Weeping Woman. Sunstone Press, 2011.

Bellanger, Jeff. World's Most Haunted Places. The Rosen Publishing Group, 2009.

Birnes, William J. Aliens in America: A UFO Hunter's Guide to Extraterrestrial Hot Spots Across the U.S. Adams Media, 2010.

Blackwood, Algernon. The Wendigo. VII, Start Publishing, 2013.

Calu, John. Mystery of the Jersey Devil. iUniverse, 2005.

Coleman, Loren. Mothman and Other Curious Encounters. Cosimo Inc., 2001

Cox, William T. Fearsome Animals of the Lumberwoods: With a few desert and mountain beasts. Press of Judd & Detwiler Inc., 1910.

Francis, Scott. Monster Spotter's Guide to North America. Monsters of the Midwest, F&W Media, 2007.

Hall, Mark A. & Rollins, Mark L. Thunderbirds: America's Living Legends of Giant Birds. Cosimo Inc., 2008.

Hamilton, Sue L. Ghosts and Goblins. ABDO, 2010.

Moran, Mark & Mark Sceurman. Weird U.S.: Your Travel Guide to America's Local Legends and Best Kept Secrets. Sterling Publishing Company, 2009.

Morphy, Rob. Giant Space Brains of Palos Verdes (California, USA) American Monsters. Web. 16 Jan. 2011.

Radford, Benjamin. Tracking the Chupacabra: The Vampire Beast in Fact, Fiction, and Folklore. UNM Press, 2011.

Renner, James. It Came From Ohio: True Tales of the Weird, Wild, and Unexplained. Gray & Company Publishers, 2012.

Salisbury, Francis B. The Utah UFO Display: A Scientist Brings Reason and Logic to Over 400 UFO Sightings in Utah's Uintah Basin. Cedar Fort, 2010.

Scuerman, Mark & Moran, Mark. Weird N.J.: Your Travel Guide to New Jersey's Local Legends and Best Kept Secrets. Sterling Publishing Company, 2009.

Sceurman, Mark, et al. Weird U.S.: The Odd-yssey Continues: Your Travel Guide to America's Local Legends and Best Kept Secrets. Sterling Publishing Company, 2008.

Souliere, Michelle. What Monsters Roam the Maine woods? Strange Maine: True Tales from the Pine Tree State. The History Press, 2011.

Waldin, Dave in Bahr, J. et al. Weird Virginia: Your Travel Guide to Virginia's Local Legends and Best Kept Secrets. Sterling Publishing Company, 2007.

# AFTERWORD

With the *States of Terror* series, we hope to shed light on the monster stories of the fifty states in order to better understand both them and the places they come from. Despite often being ridiculous or impossible, these stories persist for a reason, as a shared heritage of people and places. They represent unique fears, urges, and prejudices as varied as the country itself.

Like a kid around the campfire to whom the opportunity to conjure a story has been passed, we're reimagining these tales in order to see them anew. Our hopes for this book, and for future volumes, is for readers to become inspired by our renditions, to seek out others, and to keep the memory of these monsters—and their creators—alive and terrifying for many years to come.

Of course, none of this would have been possible without the energy and enthusiasm of our contributors —a weird band of (mostly) west coast writers and (mostly) east coast artists, brought together by a sheer joy for dabbling in the arcane corners of American folklore. Working with them has been quite a ride, and we hope it's not the last one.

As you can see, we've still got a lot of states to go...and the going is sure to get weirder.

—M.L. & K.M.

Made in the USA
Charleston, SC
06 March 2016